Slow Ride

Sleeper Seals, Book 2

Becky McGraw

Acknowledgements

This book is dedicated to Eileen, my amazing go-to for all things Navy related, including hot SEALs, and to Carolyn, my editor, steadfast friend, and book-writing rudder. Thank you both for your friendship and sage advice.

SLOW RIDE, Copyright © 2017 by Becky McGraw.
ISBN-13: 978-1977573834
ISBN-10: 1977573835

Cover Photo Credit: Photographer: © 2017, Jules Godfrey Photography, Cover Model: Jack Dutton, Cover Designer: Becky McGraw, Cover Me Photography & Design

Becky McGraw Books
PO Box 144
Bagdad, Florida 32530

Ordering Information:
Quantity sales. Special discounts are available on quantity purchases by corporations, associations, and others. For details, contact the publisher at the address above.

Printed in the United States of America

PROLOGUE

Retired Navy Commander Greg Lambert leaned forward to rake in the pile of chips his full house had netted him. Tonight he would leave the weekly gathering not only with his pockets full, but his pride intact.

The scowls he earned from his poker buddies at his unusual good luck was an added bonus.

They'd become too accustomed to him coming up on the losing side of five card stud. It was about time he taught them to never underestimate him.

Vice President Warren Angelo downed the rest of his bourbon and stubbed out his Cuban cigar. "Looks like Lady Luck is on your side tonight, Commander."

After he neatly stacked his chips in a row at the rail in front of him, Greg glanced around at his friends. It occurred to him right then, this weekly meeting wasn't so different from the joint sessions they used to have at the Pentagon during his last five years of service.

The location was the Secretary of State's basement now, but the gathering still included top ranking military brass, politicians, and the director of the CIA, who had been staring at him strangely all night long.

"It's about time the bitch smiled my way, don't you think? She usually just cleans out my pockets and gives you my money," Greg replied with a sharp laugh as his eyes roved over the spacious man-cave with envy, before they snagged on the wall clock.

It was well past midnight, their normal break-up time. He needed to get home, but what did he have to go home to? Four walls, and Karen's mean-as-hell

Chihuahua who hated him. Greg stood, scooted back his chair, and stretched his shoulders. The rest of his poker buddies quickly left, except for Vice President Angelo, Benedict Hughes with the CIA, and their host tonight, Percy Long, the Secretary of State.

He took the last swig of his bourbon, then set the glass on the table. When he took a step to leave, they moved to block his way to the door. "Something on your minds, gentleman?" he asked, their cold, sober stares making the hair on the back of his neck stand up.

It wasn't a comfortable feeling, but one he was familiar with from his days as a Navy SEAL. That feeling usually didn't portend anything good was about to go down. But neither did the looks on these men's faces.

Warren cleared his throat and leaned against the mahogany bar with its leather trimmings. "There's been a significant amount of chatter lately." He glanced at Ben. "We're concerned."

Greg backed up a few steps, putting some distance between himself and the men. "Why are you telling me this? I've been out of the loop for a while now." Greg was retired, and bored stiff, but not stiff enough to tackle all that was wrong in the United States at the moment, or fight the politics involved in fixing things.

Ben let out a harsh breath then gulped down his glass of water. He set the empty glass down on the bar with a sigh and met Greg's eyes. "We need your help, and we're not going to beat around the bush," he said, making Greg's short hairs stand taller.

2

Greg put his hands in his pockets, rattling the change in his right pocket and his car keys in the left while he waited for the hammer. Nothing in Washington, D.C. was plain and simple anymore. Not that it ever had been.

"Spit it out, Ben," he said, eyeballing the younger man. "I'm all ears."

"Things have changed in the US. Terrorists are everywhere now," he started, and Greg bit back a laugh at the understatement of the century.

He'd gotten out before the recent CONUS attacks started, but he was still in service on 9/11 for the ultimate attack. The day that replaced Pearl Harbor as the day that would go down in infamy.

"That's not news, Ben," Greg said, his frustration mounting in his tone. "What does that have to do with me, other than being a concerned citizen?"

"More cells are being identified every day," Ben replied, his five o'clock shadow standing in stark contrast to his now paler face. "The chatter about imminent threats, big jihad events that are in the works, is getting louder every day."

"You do understand that I'm no longer active service, right?" Greg shrugged. "I don't see how I can be of much help there."

"We want you to head a new division at the CIA," Warren interjected. "Black Ops, a sleeper cell of SEALs to help us combat the terrorist sleeper cells in the US…and whatever the hell else might pop up later."

3

Greg laughed. "And where do you think I'll find these SEALs to sign up? Most are deployed over—"

"We want retired SEALs like yourself. We've spent millions training these men, and letting them sit idle stateside while we fight this losing battle alone is just a waste." Ben huffed a breath. "I know they'd respect you when you ask them to join the contract team you'd be heading up. You'd have a much better chance of convincing them to help."

"Most of those guys are like me, worn out to the bone or injured when they finally give up the teams. Otherwise, they'd still be active. SEALs don't just quit." Unless their wives were taken by cancer and their kids were off at college, leaving them alone in a rambling house when they were supposed to be traveling together and enjoying life.

"What kind of threats are you talking about?" Greg asked, wondering why he was even entertaining such a stupid idea.

"There are many. More every day. Too many for us to fight alone," Ben started, but Warren held up his palm.

"The President is taking a lot of heat. He has three and a half years left in his term, and taking out these threats was a campaign promise. He wants the cells identified and the terror threats eradicated quickly."

These three, and the President, sat behind desks all day. They'd never been in a field op before, so they had no idea the planning and training that took place before a team ever made it to the field. Training a team of broken down SEALs to work together would take double that time because each knew better than the rest how things should be done, so there was no "quick" about it.

"That's a tall order. I can't possibly get a team of twelve men on the same page in under a year. Even if I can find them." Why in the hell was he getting excited, then? "Most are probably out enjoying life on a beach somewhere." Exactly where he would be with Karen if she hadn't fucking died on him as soon as he retired four years ago.

"We don't want a team, Greg," Percy Long corrected, unfolding his arms as he stepped toward him. "This has to be done stealthily because we don't want to panic the public. If word got out about the severity of the threats, people wouldn't leave their homes. The press would pump it up until they created a frenzy. You know how that works."

"So let me get this straight. You want individual SEALs, sleeper guys who agree to be called up for special ops, to perform solo missions?" Greg asked, his eyebrows lifting. "That's not usually how they work."

"Unusual times call for unusual methods, Greg. They have the skills to get it done quickly and quietly," Warren replied, and Greg couldn't argue. That's exactly the way SEALs operated—they did whatever it took to get the job done.

Ben approached him, placed his hand on his shoulder as if this was a tag-team effort, and Greg had no doubt that it was just that. "Every terrorist or wanna-be terror organization has roots here now. Al Qaeda, The Muslim Brotherhood, Isis, the Taliban—you name it. They're not here looking for asylum. They're actively recruiting followers and planning events to create a caliphate on our home turf. We can't let that happen, Greg, or the United States will never be the same."

"You'll be a contractor, so you can name your price," Warren inserted, and Greg's eyes swung to him. "You'll be on your own in the decision making. We need to have plausible deniability if anything goes wrong."

"Of course," Greg replied, shaking his head. If anything went south, they needed a fall guy, and that would be him in this scenario. Not much different from the dark ops his teams performed under his command when he was active duty.

God, why did this stupid idea suddenly sound so intriguing? Why did he think he might be able to make it work? And why in the hell did he suddenly think it was just what he needed to break out of the funk he'd been living in for four years?

"I can get you a list of potential hires, newly retired SEALs, and the President says anything else you need," Warren continued quickly. "All we need is your commitment."

The room went silent, and Greg looked deeply into each man's eyes as he pondered a decision. What the hell did he have to lose? If he didn't agree, he'd just die a slow, agonizing death in his recliner at home. At only forty-seven and still fit, that could be a lot of years spent in that chair.

"Get me the intel, the list, and the contract," he said, and a surge of adrenaline made his knees weak.

He was back in the game.

***

Keegan MacDonald knew now why the Navy called it terminal leave, because he felt like he might indeed die of boredom working at his uncle's motorcycle shop. And it had only been eighty-nine days since he officially left the teams. He had a whole lifetime to fill, and nothing to fill it with except more of the same.

You have one more day to contest the medical discharge and fight for a staff position so you can have the surgery. Do it. Being in the Navy, but not on the teams, wouldn't be that bad.

"It would be *torture*—that's what that would be," he growled as he twisted the wrench hard.

But you were going to leave the teams voluntarily not nine months ago for a woman. You got what you wanted bud, just not the way you wanted it.

The wrench slipped off of the nut and his knuckles rapped hard against the manifold. He cursed as he dropped it and it clattered on the greasy concrete floor, then slid under the bike. Damned shoulder, he thought, rubbing it as a muscle spasmed. He couldn't even hold a wrench tight enough to turn a damned nut. How in the hell did he expect to do pull-ups or scale the wall? Even in a staff position, instead of on the teams, he'd have PT standards he'd have to meet.

7

You'll never have one-hundred percent mobility again, even with surgery. The surgery could make it worse with the scar tissue.

That's what the doctor, physical therapist, and the surgeon he consulted with all concluded. That also said, in that condition, if he stayed on the teams, he might be a danger to his teammates—which meant Keegan was done.

Eighty percent mobility was good enough for a normal life, what he'd managed with six months of rehab, but not enough to be an elite athlete, someone his brothers could depend on.

But *this* was a normal life?

With a huffed breath, he slid off of the creeper to his knees and reached for the wrench. His hand closed around the shaft, but he stayed there and shut his eyes.

You worked your ass off to get through BUD/S to get your trident, went to every hellhole on earth to get to Lt. Commander—and you're giving that up without a fight? Have the surgery—the doctors might not know everything. They don't know how hard you will work when you're determined to accomplish a goal.

Keegan groaned as his hand tightened around the wrench and it cut into his palm. This was all Cee Cee Logan's fucking fault. He should've never gone to Texas to see her. He should've never let his feelings for her go beyond their agreed upon terms, or let his fantasies convince him she felt the same. But she sure acted like she felt the same.

That stupidity cost him his career, but he was

fortunate, because it could've cost him or one of his teammates their life. His mind had been on *her,* instead of the mission to Syria he was deployed on as soon as he got back from Texas. If it hadn't been, he would have double-checked that his grenade launcher module was properly attached to his rifle before he fired.

"You okay, bud?" his uncle asked.

Keegan sighed and sat back on his heels. "No, I'm not feeling right today, Uncle Bob. I think I'm going to knock off early and ride to the beach. I'm pretty much caught up."

"Well, you better get right this weekend because we have two new custom jobs coming in on Monday," Bob replied, looking concerned.

That didn't surprise him at all because Bob MacDonald was known as the best custom bike builder on the east coast. Keegan should be thrilled to be here learning everything he could from him, so he could open his own shop one day. That was the plan, but he just couldn't find the passion he thought he'd have for it.

They'd talked about him coming to work at MacDonald Customs for years now. Keegan dreamed about it while he was deployed. It kept him sane. But now that he was doing it, it just didn't give him the satisfaction he thought it would.

Being a SEAL was the only thing he ever seemed to have a passion for in his life, and now that he wasn't one, Keegan had no idea what to do with himself. He had one more day to decide if he could deal with civilian life.

This weekend, he was going to the beach to surf and get his head right.

"A little surfing should do the trick. No worries, Unk, I'll be here on Monday in a better frame of mind." Keegan forced a smile as he stood.

"Find yourself a mermaid while you're down there. *That's* what you need, Son," his uncle said with a wink and a hearty laugh.

A woman was the last thing he needed right now.

"You know it. That's on the list right under surfing." *And a lobotomy.*

Blowing out a breath, Keegan walked to the back of the shop and out the back door. He strode across the rear lot to the trailer he temporarily called home. Ninety days and he was still in the twenty-foot travel trailer.

"*Stop* it!" he shouted, as he grabbed the door handle and yanked it hard. Ten years of his life given to this country was enough. It was time for him to stop the pity party and figure this shit out. He was going to do that this weekend.

After a quick shower, Keegan filled his go bag with board shorts and tanks. He tossed his phone inside and zipped it up, but as soon as he picked up the bag, his phone rang. With a growl, he set it back down and fished it out. An unfamiliar number showed on the display, but he recognized the DC area code, so he thought it might be something to do with his forced retirement.

"This is MacDonald," he grumbled.

"Lieutenant Commander Keegan MacDonald?" a deep voice, repeated. The fact that he included Keegan's soon to be former title told him this was a related call.

"Yes, for now," Keegan replied, pushing it past the knot in his throat. Who the hell was he without that title and SEAL behind his name?

"This is Commander Greg Lambert. I've seen your medical report and believe you can still perform a service for your county, so I have a proposition for you."

CHAPTER ONE

"Bike's coming along nicely," Bob said, and Keegan flashed his uncle a smile that felt strange on his face. Smiling wasn't something he'd done a lot of lately.

Thank God he'd undertaken this project on his bike or he'd likely be in a rubber room right now. Being led on was something he'd had just about enough of. First by Cee Cee Logan, then by Commander Greg Lambert and his, evidently fictional, counter-terror division staffed by former SEALs he'd recruited.

There'd been plenty of terror to go around in the United States in the last eight months, but the Commander had been on radio silence since that first call. Keegan had come to the conclusion that either he had been blowing his BDUs up with smoke, or he'd placed him on the B-team due to his injury, in which case he'd never be called up unless there was nobody else. With every day that passed, his certainty of that grew, as did his feeling of uselessness.

"Just have to scoop out the middle, change the seat and I'll be done. I won't be needing a two-seater anymore, since I've sworn off women," Keegan said, tracing his fingers over the shiny black Bonefrog decal he'd applied to the side of the black, powder-coated tank.

"Sure doesn't seem like you have. How many women have you been through since you've been home?" Bob asked with a laugh.

"Just two, but that's enough to drive home the fact that I'm better off alone," Keegan replied. After he crashed and burned with Cecilia, *one* should've been enough. But, ever the optimist, Keegan just had to try again. He was now at the bottom of his optimism barrel and ready for a dry spell.

"You're too damned young to decide that—just take a break," Bob said, then harrumphed. "When you stop shopping at the beach bar bargain basement because you're desperate, the perfect woman will find you."

"Perfect and woman are two words that don't fit together, Unk, and the only thing I'm desperate to do is stay away from them right now." *And get the hell out of here, so I can skip this pep talk you're winding up to give me.*

"I have to disagree. Louise MacDonald is just about the most perfect woman in the world and she found me during a streak of bad luck in Atlantic City."

"You're right, Aunt Louise is one of a kind, and perfect for you, Uncle Bob. But I'm not looking for that complication in my already fucked-up life," Keegan said, unable to hide his irritation. "I have enough on my mind right now."

He loved his uncle unconditionally, but the pep talks and lectures since he'd been home were grating on his last nerve. Keegan just wanted to be left alone to deal with the funk he found himself in at the moment.

"This pity party of yours has got to stop. You are still a useful young man, Keegan. You just need to quit feeling sorry for yourself and get plugged back into life. There is life after the military—trust me, I know."

His uncle was right. Keegan needed to just face the bitter fact he was done as a special operator. All the blood, sweat and tears he'd put into that grueling training was now as useful to him and the government as the tarnishing medals in his dresser drawer.

Being a grease monkey at his uncle's motorcycle shop was his life now, unless he wanted to use his business degree to become a desk jockey, where he could crawl into a desk drawer and die. Because he'd let a woman distract him, and this was the price of that error in judgment.

"I think I'm going surfing this weekend," Keegan said standing, trying to push the negativity and anger from his mind.

The beach was the only panacea for him these days and he needed it right now. Out on his board finding waves, the world couldn't touch him and the waves washed away thoughts of anything other than balancing on his board.

"Aren't you waterlogged yet, boy?" Bob asked.

"Nah, I'm a frog, Unk. I belong in the water."

Was a frog, Keegan thought, grinding his teeth. Now, he was nothing but useless driftwood washed up on the beach.

"Well, think about this while you're gone. Aunt Louise has decided she wants me to retire and travel. I told her I need one more year to make sure things were set here. You're on deck when that happens—if you get your head right and want it, that is."

Shock rocked him and Keegan's mouth opened, but no words came out. *Is this what he wanted for the rest of his life?*

He had no freaking idea what he wanted, but he knew what he didn't want—a nine-to-five office job. Turning wrenches was boring, but a helluva lot more exciting than that alternative.

You wanted a shop of your own, and he's offering you that opportunity.

Uncle Bob had the reputation, but his operation was limited because he was a one-man-and-one-mechanic-band, until Keegan came home.

You'll be the boss—have the freedom to push this operation to the next level. To do far out custom bikes, dream bikes, like yours is now. This could be huge.

Keegan had an endless supply of SEAL brothers who might consider joining him when they left the teams. If there was one skill all SEALs possessed, it was being mechanically inclined and able to solve problems with machinery. The dark clouds inside his head parted as his excitement at the possibilities built.

Bob's smile slipped and he squeezed Keegan's shoulder. "Just think about it. Maybe this was just a stopping off point for you and that's fine. You need to do what makes you happy."

"*No*, Unk!" Keegan shouted, finally finding his voice. "That is an incredible offer. I was just shocked you offered it to *me*!" He thought the only way they'd ever take Bob out of this shop was toes up when he was ninety and slipped on an oil puddle.

Bob shrugged. "You're the closest thing I have to

a son and a helluva lot more responsible than your younger brother. I figure at thirty-three, next year you'll be ready, if you can get past this shit and realize you're not washed up. You still have plenty of living to do, boy."

Then why did he feel so dead inside? Because Bob was right again. Wallowing in self-pity was not improving his situation at all. He should be thankful he had his uncle and aunt on his team and that, even though he'd been a grumpy bastard lately, they were still there for him.

This weekend he would work on changing his attitude. The grumpy bastard would still be reserved for women, though, because with this added responsibility, he certainly didn't need that distraction.

"Thank you, Uncle Bob. You have no idea how much this means to me."

"Just keep doing what you're doing, so I don't change my mind. Louise would kill me," he said with a rough laugh.

Keegan's phone vibrated in his pocket and traveled down his hipbone. He pulled it out, looked at the display and groaned. *Now? Really?* He ought to just let it ring to voicemail, but he couldn't resist answering, if for nothing more than to tell him to go to hell.

"This is MacDonald. I was wondering if you'd forgotten about me, Commander," Keegan said, unable to keep the anger from his tone.

"Definitely not. I just didn't need you, but I do now. Are you available for a mission?" Greg Lambert asked. Keegan tried to hang onto his anger but excitement washed it away.

"I signed up for them, you're paying me a stipend to be available, so yes, I'm at your disposal," he replied, sucking in a breath to control the rush of adrenaline that swamped him.

"Good—I need you to—" Lambert started.

"Wait—let me find somewhere private to talk." With a chin nod, he left his uncle standing there to walk-run toward the back door. He flung open the door and hustled across the back lot to the little tin can he lived in and went inside. "Okay, I'm secure—what do you have?"

After Bob's little revelation, Keegan didn't know how he'd take the news of him taking off indefinitely on a mission at the spur of the moment. He'd probably think he was as irresponsible as Kane, his younger brother. But this man paid him a monthly retainer, he'd committed to taking missions, and he would. He'd just tell Bob he'd been called up for a special reserve training drill.

"I need you to go Little Creek and do recon at the strip club near the back gate. Someone is passing top secret and classified information to the enemy at the Lily Pad and I need to you find out who that is."

"What kind of information? Which enemy?" Keegan asked.

"Counter-intelligence regarding the war on terror is being passed to ISIS and Al Qaeda sympathizers who frequent that bar." Greg huffed a breath. "The latest leak resulted in two SEAL teams being ambushed and ten men killed on what should've been an easy operation. We've had three ISIS and two Al Qaeda inside operatives beheaded in the last few months. We won't be able to keep the other friendlies, if this isn't stopped. They're scared."

"How do you know the leak is originating at that bar?" Keegan asked.

"You don't want to know that. I don't want to know that," Greg replied with a laugh. "Suffice it to say, the CIA has ways of making captured detainees talk. They believe men from the base could be involved, which makes me sick."

"Are you sure this is good intel?" Keegan had been in so many situations in the sandbox where it wasn't, he had to ask. Men got killed relying on bad information and he wasn't going to be one of them.

"The FBI has verified there's a leak and that it's *most likely* originating at that club. Because of the classification and nature of the information being passed, they believe a SEAL from the base would be a likely source. That's all they have because they don't have the manpower to handle the investigation properly, which is why we're on deck…or you are."

"Do they have names of the men on base?" Keegan asked, because that would give him a leg-up on the investigation.

"No, the brass doesn't have evidence and can't go profiling, but we're not bound by those rules, so we have to look at everyone. We're basically starting from scratch here, but if a SEAL is involved, I'd like to personally *interrogate* him before you turn him over."

"I'll give you what's left of him, if that's the case, Commander," Keegan replied darkly.

The thought of a SEAL possibly being involved made him sick, too. The teams were a brotherhood, and this traitor's intentional betrayal had gotten ten of his teammates killed.

"So, you're taking the mission?" Greg asked, sounding relieved.

"Yes, sir, I'll take the mission gladly."

"Good—go to the Lily Pad Club outside of the back gate at the base and sign on as a bouncer or bar back. You'll have to get the job on your own because I can't set it up. That would give us away. Everyone there is a suspect until you weed them out."

"Yes, sir—I'll leave in the morning."

"Check in with me weekly if you can manage it, or call me if you need *anything*. I have to keep God apprised of what's going on."

Keegan hung up the phone and a spark of excitement lit the dry brush in the wasteland that was his psyche before that call. It flamed brighter, that old feeling of usefulness, of service to a cause greater than his own, returned with a vengeance.

Keegan shot to his feet to go pack his go bag, feeling better than he had in eight months.

Maybe he could have his cake and eat it too, he thought, flinging open the trailer door to go find his uncle to tell him he was going on a reserve training mission.

CHAPTER TWO

Jules scrubbed at a large sticky spot on a table near the stage, the origin of which she didn't want to identify. Thank God she had a supply of rubber gloves in her locker, because there was plenty in this bar she didn't want to touch with her bare hands, including the patrons. But she at least had to try and make things cleaner, because after three months the filth was driving her nuts.

Her boss, Frank, needed to hire a cleaning staff who cared, because she was about done serving as both a waitress and a maid. Two-dollars and ten cents an hour didn't buy him both and the Lily Pad was about the most disgusting place she'd ever worked.

"Nice *ass*," someone said behind her with a phlegmy laugh. Jules shivered, and scrubbed at the spot harder. "You should be up there on stage, sweetness. I'd pay good money to see that."

She glanced back over her shoulder to stare into the road-mapped eyes of Benny, a regular who was as disgusting as the bar.

"Start by tipping me on the floor, Benny, and we'll talk," she growled, slapping her rag down on her tray as he crowded up behind her to sit down in a chair. *Touch me, bastard, and you'll be staring up at me from the floor.*

The degenerate had been kicked out of the bar on more than one occasion for getting touchy-feely with the waitresses and strippers. Jules wanted to kick him in the balls to give him a wakeup call as he stared down her cleavage licking his lips, but she just gave him a tight smile before walking toward the bar.

Working in this place had sure given her a different perspective on men and on humanity, just when she thought it was as low as it could ever be. The front door opened and bright sunshine backlit a large body that stood in the doorway. From the bulk, she suspected the body of the shadow man belonged to a SEAL.

If she never saw another one of those arrogant, testosterone-filled assholes again, she'd count herself lucky. Jules loved alpha men, appreciated their service to the country, but they pushed the envelope. Some were true heroes both on and off duty, but the ones who came here were single and looking to let their hair down to the toes of their combat boots. Add naked women and a lot of alcohol to that mix, and they definitely lost the halos and their inhibitions.

Lost in thought, Jules slammed right into a body very unlike that of a Navy SEAL. It jiggled and beefy hands squeezed her breasts hard. Before she could drop her tray to drop the pervert who'd grabbed her, he flew away from her and was slammed to the ground. A big, combat-booted foot pressed down on the center of his throat and he whimpered.

"Apologize to the lady, or die, buddy. Your choice." Her eyes landed on hammer-like fists which were ready at his sides and followed the myriad of tattoos up rock-hard, veined arms to a thick neck and a hard profile.

Maybe the guy who just arrived wasn't a SEAL after all. He looked more like a biker with his shaggy hair and tats, and sounded like one too. The delicious, bulging

21

muscles definitely said military man, but that was the only thing about him that did.

Whatever and whoever he was, she was thankful to see him, because Trace, their bouncer, hadn't even noticed Ron moving in. He was too busy sitting on his perch by the front door, flirting with a woman who had to be a SEAL groupie, a frog hog.

Movement at the end of the bar caught her attention and she watched her boss Frank lift the bar window and walk out, his face ruddy and determined. She knew what that meant—he was about to throw both of them out on their ass. Before he could, Jules hopped over the man on the floor to put her hand into Frank's chest.

"Ron grabbed my tits again, Frankie—that guy saw it and was helping me, not starting trouble," she said, but his eyes traveled over her shoulder.

"Sure looks like a troublemaker to me. Beat it— *both* of you or I'm calling the cops," Frank growled, wiping his hands on a bar towel.

"No, I'm *saving* you from trouble," the biker said, as he removed his foot from Ron's throat and took a step back. Ron quickly rolled to his side, then pushed up to his feet to walk-run toward the door. "Your trouble would come if word got out on base this place is a common nuisance and the COs restrict the guys from coming here. Add in a civil suit from her for not providing adequate workplace security, and you could find yourself in a *heap* of trouble."

Definitely a *former* SEAL, and one who could give

22

lessons in delivering a threat, Jules thought, biting back a laugh when Frank's face went white. Nobody scared Frank, but the fear on his face was real. Frank's eyes narrowed and he put a fist on his hip.

"What are you, a fucking attorney? You gonna be the one filing that suit?" he growled.

"No, I'm a former SEAL who has plenty of friends still on base," he replied, verifying her suspicions. "I just want to make sure their interests are protected when they come here."

"What do you want from me, asshole?" Frank growled, his eyebrows crashing together.

"I want you to get rid of the asshole at the door you're paying to flirt, and reinforce your security with someone with a brain that isn't in his jockstrap," he replied.

"Reinforce my security, huh? With who—*you*?" Frank asked with a snigger, giving him a once over.

"Why not?" the man asked with a shrug. "I was paying attention when your guy wasn't. When bouncers don't pay attention things can get ugly real fast, especially here."

Frank threw his chin up and drilled the guy with his eyes. "Why should I hire you? You have thirty seconds."

"I know your clientele and what to look for—how to handle them if they get out of line. That's all you need to know."

"Why are you a *former* SEAL if you're so badass?"

Frank shot back.

"Because I let a woman distract me, which means I have no interest in the ones who work here, or the frog hogs who hang out here. Been there, done that, and the t-shirt doesn't fit anymore," the man replied gruffly.

With the delicious muscles on display from his black tank top, Jules could definitely see the t-shirt not fitting. But his statement made her wonder about the woman. What kind of woman would catch this man's eye, or better yet, be interesting enough to distract him to the point of sacrificing a career he had to work his ass off to achieve?

Frank studied him a minute longer, then turned and strode to the front door. Evidently Trace still didn't notice there was trouble. Even when it walked right in the front door, Jules thought, folding her arms over her chest to watch the show.

"Trace—you're *fired*!" Frank shouted, stopping in front of the bouncer.

That finally got the desired reaction. Trace's head spun on his shoulders and his mouth flapped, before his eyes narrowed.

"Are you serious? What the hell for?" he asked, sliding off the stool to glare down at Frank who was six inches shorter and probably seventy pounds lighter.

Slow and stealthily, the man who was their new bouncer glided to stand by the door behind Frank. He didn't rush in or crowd Frank, he just stood there and she knew why. He was telling Trace, without saying a word, that he had Frank's back, or in SEAL terms, his six.

Jules jumped when the music suddenly blared, telling her it was *show* time. Although she'd thoroughly enjoyed watching the scene at the door, she had work to do and people to watch. Tonight, though, she would probably be watching the new bouncer more than anyone, because his convenient grand entrance into her nasty little world had piqued her curiosity.

CHAPTER THREE

Keegan picked out the top of the blonde waitress's head as she pushed her way through the throng of men blocking her way to the bar to make sure idle hands didn't find her delectable ass before she made it there. That skimpy costume, which pushed up her amazing rack and did nothing to cover her backside, was the common nuisance here.

He knew before this job was done, he would end up being mostly *her* bodyguard. At least on the stage, the strippers could get away from the hands that reached for them. She was right in the middle of things, and took the brunt of the sexual advances the strippers incited.

What kind of woman would choose to work in a place like this? Yeah, she probably made amazing tips with that body, but she must be desperate for money to choose this.

The shrill whine of a fire alarm introduced a new act and his eyes moved to the two poles at center stage just as two strippers dressed in turnout coats and fire hats appeared. Twins, if he wasn't mistaken, or women who looked enough alike to be mistaken for twins. Every man's fantasy, except for him, it seemed. Keegan only wanted one woman at a time, but that was even too much at the moment.

He *must* be getting old, because as he sat there watching them feel up their own bodies and bump and grind to the music, it did nothing for him. He wondered how he'd ever found this titillating. He couldn't judge, though, because back in his tadpole days, he'd been right there with the guys at that stage, drinking and drooling. With enough liquor in him back then, he'd have probably thought his third grade teacher was hot, if she showed up on stage.

Tonight, he had no liquor on board, and at thirty-two years old, those women looked like hard-plastic caricatures of real women. His hard-living days lusting after hard-plastic woman were as over as his career.

"Hi, I'm Jules," a feminine voice shouted and Keegan looked down into the blue eyes of the waitress he'd 'saved' to get this job. She tucked her tray under her arm to stick out her hand to him. "I just wanted to say thank you for stepping in with Ron, earlier. He's a pain in the ass."

Jules definitely wasn't plastic, he thought, his eyes fixing on her lush, very real breasts as he took her hand and a tingle zipped up his arm.

"Keegan MacDonald and you're welcome," he replied, pulling her closer so she could hear him. He sniffed and curled his nose when the smell of stale booze and cigarette smoke assaulted his senses.

The smell of this bar had evidently soaked into her shiny, golden hair and he wondered what she'd smell like when she wasn't here. If she worked here long enough, that scent might become permanent and that was too bad.

He hoped she could find something else to do to earn a living so it didn't happen, but why he cared was beyond him. With a laugh, she pulled her hand from his and wiped it on the bottom of her uniform.

"It's nice to meet you, Keegan. I wondered if I could buy you breakfast to thank you when we get off? There's a place within walking distance," she said, and her bright, white smile framed by full, red lips punched him in the gut.

"No need, but thanks for the offer," he replied, wondering if she was coming on to him.

She had some powerful tools if so, because although he had zero interest in women right now, his body was definitely interested. He bit back a growl when he realized he was doing the same thing his predecessor had done to get fired, and he was letting this woman distract him while he was on a mission. His shoulder ached, and he reached up to rub it.

"Please? I'd really like to get to know you and there's no way that can happen here," she insisted, swiping her blonde hair from her forehead with her wrist.

"*Jules*! Order up!" Frank shouted from the bar with enough volume to cut through the loud music and chatter. She looked back over her shoulder and rolled her eyes.

"I'll talk to you later when the crowd thins out a little." She turned and Keegan's eyes locked on her beautiful ass, which was only covered by fishnet hose and a triangle of material that thinned to the red string that disappeared between her cheeks. She looked as good coming as she did going, he thought, and his dick went rock-hard.

With a growl, Keegan dragged his eyes back to the elbow-to-elbow crowd. This mission might not be as easy as he thought, if this was a typical crowd size. But it was Thursday night, ladies' night, and there were plenty of frog hogs in the mob.

That meant there were also plenty of guys from the base here for him to catalog, but too many red herring civilians too. Telling them apart when all of them were in street clothes would be impossible. He had a feeling the turd he was looking for would float to the top when things weren't so busy, so he'd be patient. Passing information in this mosh pit would be almost impossible. In all likelihood, it was being done when the bar wasn't so busy.

Keegan stood to give some blood flow to his ass, which had gone numb sitting on the stool by the door for hours. He stretched his arms over his head to work the stiffness from his shoulders, then looked toward the stage. Air rushed from his lungs as he lowered his arms and pushed his way into the crowd to go check out things near the stage.

Once inside the mass of bodies, he was glad to be over six foot tall so he could see where he was going. He couldn't imagine how the much shorter waitresses, including his new friend *Jules*, could do this with drinks on a tray.

Keegan was thankful to have on steel-toed boots, because he counted at least ten times his toes were stepped on during his journey to the front. Two rows back, a drunk staggered into him and he gave the man a hard push. The crowd parted and he could finally get to the stage.

Surveying the seven tables lining the stage, he found nothing interesting until the last one on the end, where he saw Jules serving drinks to four military guys. One seemed to be taking a pretty keen interest in her so Keegan stayed there to watch.

Sure enough, that man grabbed her arm and pulled her closer to whisper in her ear, but she jerked away and shook her head. He didn't take no for an answer, though, he slid a chair up behind her then pushed her into the seat.

Keegan lunged in that direction, but the guy suddenly doubled over when Jules landed an elbow in his gut, then doubled down with a quick backhanded punch to his nose. Good for her, he thought, shoving through the last two guys blocking him.

She was on her feet when Keegan stopped at the table, but the look on her assailant's face said the fight wasn't over as he swiped blood from under his nose. His buddies roared and he scraped back his chair to stand. Jules dropped her tray and assumed a martial arts defensive stance that Keegan knew well.

What he wanted to know was how *she* knew it. Was she former military too?

That pose wouldn't be helping her in this fight, though—that guy was six foot five at least and could pound her right into the ground. The man rushed her and her knee found his crotch as her fist slammed into his ear. The blow took him to his knees, but he was still almost her height on his knees and he wasn't out.

He grabbed her legs, pulled her feet from under her and she landed hard on her back. Before she could roll, he pounced on her just as Keegan got there. Fisting the man's t-shirt, he yanked him back hard, and glared down at him. Chairs scraped back behind him, but he didn't look away.

"Stay out of it, or you'll get your ass kicked too," he growled, before pulling the guy on the floor up closer. "Wanna pick on someone your own size, asshole? Or is your dick not big enough for that?" The kid, who sported a high and tight, was probably fresh out of boot camp. He squirmed to break the hold, but Keegan reeled him in tighter. "If you ever want to be allowed back in here, I suggest you apologize to the lady, before I throw you out."

"I'm not apologizing to that *bit*—" he started, but Keegan twisted the shirt tighter around his throat so he couldn't finish the sentence.

"If you don't want to go to jail tonight, you will, kid," he growled. "The owner has called the police and I'm sure the lady will want to press charges. I'll bet your CO might serve you a big ole chicken dinner if that happens, huh?" A bad conduct discharge would be this asshole's ticket home and to a lifetime of embarrassment explaining in civilian life why he received it.

"Let me go and I'm out of here," the kid

31

squeaked, scuffing his boots to try to stand again.

"*Not* until you apologize," Keegan repeated shoving him back down.

"I'm *sorry!*" he grated, trying to pry Keegan's fingers from his shirt.

When Keegan released him and stepped back, the kid scrambled to his feet and glared at him as he rubbed his throat. His eyes said he wanted to fight and his fists did too, but evidently the kid had a brain after all, because he just shoulder nudged him as he pushed past him to walk toward the front door.

He turned back to the table where the kid's three buddies, probably also full of testosterone now that they were out of boot camp, sat looking a little shell-shocked.

"If you're going to come here, you will show respect to the staff. No touching the servers or the dancers—got that?" Keegan felt like he was a kindergarten teacher at the moment, and he didn't like it because it made him feel old.

"Yes, sir," they all three said in unison.

He turned and saw Jules was still on the floor. "Are you okay?" he asked moving behind her to put his hands under her arms to help her up. He tensed when his hand closed over a small holster under her arm.

"Yes, I twisted my ankle when I fell, but otherwise I'm fine," she replied, as he helped her up to her feet.

"That's two times I saved you today, so breakfast *is* on you," he whispered into her ear as he dropped his hands to his sides and stepped back. *Because I want to get to know you better too—and find out why you are carrying a weapon in this bar.*

That wasn't allowed with just a regular concealed-carry permit and could get her serious time if she was caught. He needed to remind her of that. Yeah, he had his pistol in a boot holster, but he had a military carry permit, for as long as he remained on the SEAL contractor team.

A flash of red caught his eye as one of the strippers on stage whisked away the top of her red-sequined bikini. He watched her nod at a guy in the shadows at the end of the stage and walk that way. The man took her hand to help her down the stairs, then led her to a room almost out of view behind the stage.

"What's back there?" Keegan asked, his eyebrows drawing together.

"Private dance rooms," Jules responded.

Keegan brushed past her to go see for himself, because that would be a prime place for a meeting between traitors to pass information. He might need to requisition audio surveillance equipment from the commander for those rooms, if he could find a way to install it without being caught.

He stopped outside the first room and did a quick peep inside the window on the door to assess the situation. When he saw the occupants weren't watching the door, he took a second, longer look. A man who appeared to be middle-eastern sat in a lounge chair, while a brunette stripper gave him an enthusiastic lap dance.

Keegan couldn't see either of their faces well—just flashes of the man's face when she moved—which frustrated him.

"That's Ari, he's a regular. He comes in once or twice a week to see Ruby for a private lap dance." Keegan turned to look down at Jules, who he hadn't realized was by his side.

"Last name?" he asked.

"No idea—we don't ask for last names here," she replied.

"*We?* Are you a *we* here, *Jules?*" he asked staring down into her eyes, because he knew the answer but wanted confirmation.

She was here doing the same thing *he* was doing here—recon—Keegan just needed to find out for whom. Friend or foe.

CHAPTER FOUR

Jules counted down the minutes until her shift was over. She quickly cleaned up her area, then ran to the locker room to change. The strippers sat at makeup tables gabbing while they undressed and removed their makeup, but she didn't stop to chat.

Her goal was to get out of the bar as soon as possible, before the new bouncer held her to having breakfast with him. Getting cozy with him could get her information, but she could slip up too and out herself.

We? Are you a we here, Jules?

She'd let down her guard and that could get her killed if she wasn't careful. Something was up with that brooding man and she needed to keep her distance until she figured out what that was. *Keegan MacDonald.* Possibly former SEAL, but also probable agent for someone.

He said he'd left the teams because of a woman. Was he dishonorably discharged? Did he have a vendetta against the military? Or had her SAIC sent someone inside to help her without telling her? So far, Brand Carter seemed like a conscientious boss, so she doubted that was the case. That meant Keegan MacDonald was working for someone else, possibly the radical Islamists or sympathizers she was trying to weed out here.

As soon as she got to her apartment, she would text her boss and ask for everything she could get on him. When she at least knew something about MacDonald, she would covertly interrogate him to pinpoint his reason for being at the club. He *had* a reason for being there without a doubt. His appearance today and method of getting hired at the Lily Pad were too coincidental.

Jules sat down on the bench in front of her locker and sighed as she took off her heels. She raised her foot to prop it on the bench and rub her sore ankle. It was swollen, but not dramatically. Thank goodness she hadn't broken it when that drunk bastard fell on her.

"Stupid, drunken asshole," she mumbled, as she dropped her foot to the floor to stand and remove her bottoms and hose.

After this operation was over, she doubted she would ever frequent a bar again. This was a disgusting assignment, but Jules took it, because it was probably her only shot at a permanent position on the counter-intelligence team, which she'd been denied for ten years. Nobody else wanted the assignment, but she did, since it was likely the only opportunity she'd have to prove herself.

So far, she'd proven nothing except she was better suited to the white-collar crime unit she'd been assigned to for seven years. It was time for her to figure this case out, before they pulled her from it. In three months, she should've at least had something to give to Brand, but all she had were unfounded suspicions. She wasn't throwing those his way because that would just make her look stupid if she was way off base.

Jules pulled out the wad of bills in her bra and stashed them with her holster deep inside her duffle bag. She quickly shed the rest of her clothes then grabbed a bottle of body wash, shampoo, a towel, and her shower shoes, before heading to the shower.

Would she ever stop smelling like stale cigarettes and alcohol? She was almost afraid in the three months she'd been in the club that the smell had seeped into her skin so deep she'd never get rid of it. Fifteen minutes later, she dressed in her jeans and t-shirt, put on her belly band holster and slid her gun inside.

Tired as hell, she towel-dried her hair and felt marginally human again as she stashed her stuff back in her bag. And she still had six blocks to walk to the apartment the agency set up for her. Thank goodness that would be in tennis shoes instead of heels, she thought, hefting her bag onto her shoulder and cringing when she took a step on her swollen ankle.

She needed to ice it down and take ibuprofen as soon as she got home, or she wouldn't be wearing heels tomorrow night. Limping to the back door, she opened it and stepped outside then leaned against the wall to inhale deeply. She coughed and covered her nose when the odor of hot garbage from the dumpster replaced the bar smell.

Her stomach rolled as she pushed off of the wall and took a step, but the bright security lights overhead were suddenly eclipsed by a large body. The hair on her neck raised as her heart skidded to a stop and she reached under the hem of her shirt. A large hand clamped down on her wrist, holding her hand tightly to her side before she could draw her weapon.

"Are you trying to weasel out of breakfast, Jules?"

Keegan MacDonald asked, and his voice rumbling in her ears sent tingles down her neck.

"No, I'm not reneging, I'm just too tired tonight. How about a rain-check?" she asked, as his intense stare set her nerves on fire.

"It's not *night*, it's nearly three in the morning and it's not raining," he replied, as his hot breaths fanned her face and his intense energy buzzed around her. "I'm hungry, and you owe me breakfast." His eyes made it look like he was hungry for more than breakfast, and Jules body wanted to offer him a buffet at that moment.

But she didn't know anything about him, and he could be the enemy.

"Move your hands," she said, trying to slide her hand from under her shirt.

"Not until you promise not to shoot me," he replied evenly, and a burst of fear caused her legs to buckle because he obviously realized she was carrying.

"I won't shoot you if you get your hands off of me," she grated, and he smiled as his hands fell away and he took a step back.

"My question is, why are you armed inside a bar? That could buy you time in jail if you ever had reason to be frisked, since you're a civilian." he said, and his eyes raked her from head to toe. "I'm sure there would be a line for that privilege."

Jules felt like she had just had been frisked—with his eyes. Had this man made her out as an agent, or was he fishing?

38

"I think it would be obvious why I'm armed. I'm a *woman* and I work in a *titty* bar," she replied, adding an eye roll for emphasis.

"Your military martial arts training should be enough of a deterrent and a lot safer, don't you think? That costume doesn't offer many concealment opportunities, so if I noticed your hold gun, someone else will, too," he said, and that statement solidified she'd probably been made.

Fuck, fuckity, fuck. She needed to get in touch with Brand, because this was not good. If this man had ID'd her, she would be useless here now, and if he was the enemy and outed her, she could be dead.

Her eyes slid up his broad chest to meet his stare again and she found him watching her closely. An operator's standard procedure to gauge her reaction. Was it just because he was a former SEAL and trained in those techniques? Or was he an operative now for someone other than the military? His kind of skills were in high demand with terrorist organizations.

They loved to recruit disgruntled former military guys—a former SEAL would be a gold mine for them. The only way to find out for sure which side of the field he played on was to have breakfast with him. What did she have to lose at this point?

"The café is about five blocks from here," she said, stepping around him.

"I really just came back here to offer you a ride home because of your ankle. I figured you'd try to sneak out the back," he replied, grabbing her arm. "My bike is around the side of the building. Let's go."

How did he know she was on foot? That she didn't have a vehicle here? Better yet that she didn't have a boyfriend picking her up?

When she walked around the side of the building with him and he waved at Candi, who was getting into the car with her boyfriend, Blane, Jules had her answer. This man had been asking around about her with the other employees.

Definitely not good.

When he stopped beside an expensive custom bike parked at the front end of the building, Jules insides took a slow, sexy roll and her mind soared down the road on that bike. Her feet carried her toward him, and by the time she arrived, her mind was halfway to Virginia Beach.

"Wow...*that* is a *beautiful* machine, Mr. MacDonald," Jules said, awestruck as she stopped to take in the full glory of the badass Harley V-Rod Muscle with a lowered front end, black powder-coated airbox cover, billets, and pipes.

When her mind snapped back to the present, she wondered how an unemployed SEAL could afford to own such a bike. More questions that needed answers, because she immediately rejected the answer that presented. He was selling his skills to the enemy at an exorbitant price.

"This is a first. I've never had a woman lust over my bike before. I should've painted it black a long time

40

ago," he said, laughing as he held out his flat black half-shell helmet to her. "Here, wear my helmet because I don't have two."

She took the helmet, but he moved and the light reflected off of a shiny black spot on the tank and she stepped closer to run her fingers over the decal, trying to figure out what it was.

"What's this?" she asked, tracing it again.

"Bonefrog," he mumbled, as he went behind the bike and pulled a leather jacket from the saddlebag, then slid it on.

"What does it mean?" she asked, realizing it was a frog skeleton holding a triton.

"It means I'm a washed up fucking SEAL. Just put the damned helmet on—I'm tired and hungry," he growled.

Ouch. Touchy subject, which also pointed to the conclusion she didn't want to make.

He pushed the bike forward off of the stand, then cranked it. She felt the throaty sound and vibrations in her chest as she snapped the chin strap. A thrill ripped through her as she pushed her duffle to her back and stepped on the peg. He scooted forward and she threw her leg over the seat then settled behind him.

A sense of rightness soothed her as she melded her body with his, slid her arms around his trim waist and laid her face against his broad back. The scent of the smooth, well-worn leather under her cheek soothed her, his heat inflamed her and the vibrations under her titillated her.

This man was as badass as his bike, dark and dangerous. Alpha men did it for her. If they owned a bike, she was done for. This man and this bike were her ultimate fantasy.

He put the bike in gear and a rush of freedom surged through her as he zoomed across the parking lot. She could fantasize all she wanted, but Jules knew as soon as she got off this bike, she was going to have to forget this ever happened.

She was here to do a job, and this bad boy had just been added to her suspect list.

CHAPTER FIVE

"You seem like a reasonably intelligent woman. Why would you be working in a strip club as a waitress?" Keegan MacDonald asked, pinning her with a potent stare as soon as they placed their order and the waitress walked away.

"I could ask you the same thing," Jules replied, taking a sip of water straight from the less-than-clean glass the waitress left for her.

Her mouth was just that dry because all of the moisture in her body had migrated south during their short ride. The rest of it evaporated when they walked inside the bright diner and she got her first *real* look at Keegan MacDonald.

Good Lord, the former SEAL had to be the best looking man she'd ever met in a rugged, rough and ready sort of way. Just the way she liked her men. When he held the diner door and she walked past him, his body practically vibrated with sexual energy and hers hummed with awareness of that fact.

Looking into that gray-green stare was like staring into the sun, which would make focusing on getting the answers she needed difficult. Especially when she felt like he could read her mind, like those gorgeous eyes could extract every secret she held dear.

You're on an operation—this guy is a suspect until you prove otherwise.

"So, how does an unemployed SEAL afford a custom V-rod?" she asked, trying to force casualness into her tone.

"Who says I'm unemployed?" he replied, cradling his mug of black coffee. "I have a job at the bar now, so I'm not unemployed."

"That job wouldn't pay for *that* bike—" She stopped when he frowned and anger sparked in his eyes. She'd gone too far. "That was rude. I'm sorry, it's an amazing bike. Thank you for giving me a ride." *Settle down, Jules, and play the interrogation game.*

"So you like bikes?" he asked, moving the conversation back to neutral territory but his expression still wary.

"Love them," she replied, swallowing hard. "My younger brother bought a sport bike at sixteen instead of a car and let me ride it." *Six months before he killed himself and left me the bike.* Clouds gathered in her head, the pressure built behind her eyes, but Jules forced a smile. "I've had a few boyfriends with bikes too, and got hooked."

"Well, you won't be having a boyfriend with *my* bike, so don't even think of going there," he said, and shock rocked her as her chin snapped up and her face flamed.

"*Wow*—you must really think a lot of yourself, huh?" Jules asked stupefied, as her insides boiled. "You haven't got a thing to worry about there, SEAL Boy. With your attitude, you'd need a *much* better bike to spark my interest."

Jules didn't need or want a boyfriend in her life. She usually picked losers like this man, and she didn't have time for one, anyway. Arrogant bastard.

"Don't be insulted, it's not you—it's *all* women," he clarified, soothing her feathers a little, but not much.

"Are you *gay*?" she asked rather loudly, her eyes widening.

"No, I'm *not* gay," he growled, his face flushing as he looked around the restaurant.

"So why are you off of women, then?" she asked, folding her arms on the table.

"I'm just tired of the game playing that comes along with your kind and have bigger things to worry about at the moment," he replied, glaring at her.

After the boyfriends she'd had, Jules could definitely understand his mindset. She'd decided to take a break from men too. Keegan MacDonald was the first man who'd piqued her interest in a long time, and it figured he'd be on her suspect list.

That's the way things worked in her life.

"What did the woman who put you off of women do to get you kicked off the teams?" *You can either tell me, or I can find out the hard way through Brand.*

"None of your business," he grated, then fired another question at her. "How do *you* know those self-defense moves and why are you carrying a pistol inside a bar?"

It looked like they had reached a stalemate in their cross-examination. This man who was used to holding information close to his broad, muscular chest would be a tough nut to crack and she was too tired to break out her hammer. But damned if she didn't want to.

"None of *your* business," she replied, giving him a tight smile as she adopted a sing-song airhead voice. "Okay then—what shall we talk about now? Read any good books lately? What's your favorite TV show?"

"I don't watch television and I haven't had time to read a book in years, other than training manuals." He shoved a hand through his thick, dark hair. "Let's just cut to the chase, Jules—" He stopped and studied her face for a long minute, then sighed as the waitress appeared at the table with their food.

He leaned back so she could place his heaping platter of steaming scrambled eggs, hashbrowns, and half-dollar-size pancakes in front of him. She put Jules' platter of over-medium eggs and toast down in front of her then left.

Instead of picking up his fork, though, Keegan glared at her. "We can do this one of two ways. You can tell me what you're doing in that bar with a pistol, or I can tell Frank that you have it and you can explain it to him and the *police*."

Jules chewed the inside of her cheek for a second to calm down, then slid to the edge of the booth. This arrogant bastard was going to do what he'd do and nothing she said would stop him. This conversation was over, but the battle had just begun. She would find out what she needed to know about him the hard way.

"Those threats of yours might have worked on those *kids* in the bar tonight, but I can assure you they won't work on me," she said as she stood. "I'll carry my protection anywhere I see fit—so tell who you need to tell, MacDonald. Just do your *job* so I don't have to use it."

He was a lot less handsome with his face pinched as she grabbed her duffle from the seat and slung the strap over her shoulder. She turned toward the door, but his voice stopped her.

"Aren't you forgetting something, Ms. Lawson?" he asked.

"What now, Mr. MacDonald?" she asked, looking back over her shoulder.

"You need to pick up the tab before you leave," he reminded, and Jules scalp felt like it was on fire.

She plopped her bag on the table, almost in his plate, and unzipped it. She pulled out her costume so she could dig deeper for the wad of bills at the bottom. A black leather case fell out and plopped down right in the middle of his eggs. Her heart stopped as she reached for it, but he was quicker.

He leaned back to flip it open and frowned as he studied her badge. One eyebrow lifted before he snapped the case shut, wiped it off with his napkin and handed it back to her.

"*Agent* Lawson—that explains a lot."

"Interfering with a federal agent conducting an investigation is a federal offense, SEAL Boy. I'd suggest you keep that information as close to your chest as you do your own backstory, because I'd hate to have to arrest you."

"I'd like to see you try, Agent Lawson," he said, his eyes glittering. "I'm sure I'd enjoy the frisking part, but you might be the one to end up in cuffs."

"Anytime you're feeling *froggy*, we can find out," Jules shot back, as she found the wad of bills, then tucked her badge back into the bag. She slapped a twenty down beside his plate. "Just do your job, whatever *that* is, and stay out of my way, or I promise it won't end well."

"So what have you found out so far? Find the intel leak? How long have you been inside?" he asked in a hushed tone, and she froze.

What she found was the grip of her pistol and stealthily removed it from the holster. This man *was* dangerous, and he was either an operator on the same investigation as she was, or he was now her *lead* suspect.

"I have no idea what you're talking about. I'm watching Frank, because he's a tax evader," she lied, fighting to keep her face neutral but the damned tick at the corner of her mouth couldn't be stopped.

He studied her hard and those eyes of his bored into her soul, making her toes curl in her tennis shoes. "You're not a good liar, Agent Lawson, but I'm glad we're on the same team. Taking you off of my suspect list will make things easier."

Blinding anger and knee-melting relief fought for pole position inside her as she released her pistol and zipped up her bag. She leaned over his plate to put her nose near his.

48

"*Your* suspect list? This is *my* investigation, asshole. Just stand down and stay out of my way. Tell whoever you work for that I have this under control." Her blinding anger now included her new boss for not letting her know another agent was being sent in.

"If you haven't closed your investigation in three months, *Natasha*, the odds are you won't. That's probably why God sent me here," he said, giving her a cocky grin that turned her on and pissed her off at the same time.

Now, he was making fun of her? Comparing her to a cartoon secret agent? And God? He really did think a lot of himself.

"You aren't as badass as you seem to think you are, *Boris*. I had you pegged as some kind of operator when you walked through the door at the bar." She stood to cross her arms over her chest. "Your little show to get hired didn't impress or fool me one bit," she said, although now, it really did, even though she didn't want it to.

"I saved you from being mauled by a drunk—so you should be thanking me," he said, picking up his fork.

"If you didn't notice, I don't *need* your help. I had things in hand," she shot back, jerking her bag up to put the strap on her shoulder.

"No, it looked to me like the drunk had things *firmly* in hand, Natasha." He winked at her before he shoveled a forkful of scrambled eggs into his mouth and she ground her teeth.

"Enjoy your breakfast, MacDonald. I hope you

choke," she hissed.

"Good luck with your research, Lawson. Maybe we can compare notes tomorrow night to see who gets more info." The corner of his mouth curled and the bastard winked at her again, before he took a big bite out of his toast.

Jules left her breakfast behind to go home and text Brand to find out exactly who this asshole was and what he was doing in the middle of *her* investigation.

CHAPTER SIX

Frustration hitting the red zone, Jules' thumbs flew over the keypad on her phone. *What do you mean you have no idea who he is?!? He's obviously there to investigate the leak for somebody!*

The cursor blinked for almost a full minute and her eyes got dryer by the second as she stared at it. This guy couldn't be a *ghost*—someone had to know who he was and what his purpose for being at that bar was. As Special Agent in Charge, Brand Carter *should* know, but said he didn't.

Brand: *Just stay away from him and do your job.*

Jules: *I'm trying to do that, but I need to know who this guy is so I know how to handle him. He could blow my cover! Someone has to know something about his mission.*

Brand: *I'll ask around, but doubt I'll find anything. It sounds like he's special access or maybe a contractor. All I found was a lot of commendations and an honorable discharge about a year ago…but he could be a sympathizer so watch him.*

With a disgusted groan, Jules threw her phone down on the coffee table and folded her arms as her leg worked furiously, shaking the table.

Good luck with your research.

That bastard knew she wouldn't find anything on him. And now that he knew who *she* worked for, she wouldn't be finding out. She had zero leverage to make him talk.

Her phone dinged with another message and she picked it up but wanted to throw it again, when she saw a new message that had to be from *Boris*.

How's that research going, Natasha? The laughing, tear-drenched smiley that served as a period made her mouth pucker.

"How did you get my freaking agency cell phone number?" she asked aloud, as she typed in the words, adding an angry emoji.

Boris: *I have friends in high places—right next to God, as a matter of fact.* She could actually *hear* him voicing those words in that smug, sexy tone and that made her madder.

Jules: *Funny, I'd have guessed they were at the other end of that spectrum.* Why in the hell didn't they add a middle finger emoji to the lineup on her phone? She would pay extra for that.

Boris: *I say we call a truce and work on a unilateral partnership basis.*

Jules: *What kind of partnership?* The cursor blinked for a few seconds, her agitation grew and her leg started pumping again as she gripped the phone tighter.

Boris: *A unilateral partnership. You tell me everything you know and I'll see how it fits in with what I have. In turn, I'll watch your six…and I won't tell Frank what I know about you.*

Jules: *Dream on, asshole. I don't need you to watch my six, I can take care of myself. And again, if you impede my investigation, I will arrest you!*

Boris: *Considering my brother's lives are what's at stake, if you impede my investigation, you will be begging me to take you to jail by the time I finish with you.*

More threats. Her leg worked overtime now as she gritted her teeth and her fingers burned a path over the keyboard.

Jules: *You don't scare me one bit, secret squirrel. If you know what's good for you, you'll protect your nuts and leave me the hell alone.*

Her phone rang, but Jules saw it was him calling. She tossed it down on the table again and every ring gave her more satisfaction. Take that—and *smoke* it, jackass.

It was almost five o'clock, so time for her to get ready to go to the club. She stood just as sharp knuckles rapped on her door, shaking it in the frame. She stared at it and knew it had to be him. He'd probably found her address as easily as he'd gotten her phone number.

"Ride that bike back to wherever you came from, asshole!" she shouted then turned to stride toward the bathroom.

Just stay away from him and do your job. That is *exactly* what Jules was going to do.

Walking inside the bathroom, she slammed the door and shed her clothes. She was going to wash that man right out of her hair and her mind. Tonight, she would turn up the heat on this investigation. Because there was no way in hell she'd let him solve it first.

Jules leaned in and turned on the taps and kept her hand under the spray until it blended into the perfect temperature. With a sigh, she pushed back the plastic curtain and stepped inside the tub, moaning as the spray beat down on her head and heat surrounded her.

She grabbed her loofah and squirted body wash on it, then turned her back to the spray and let it massage

the tension from her shoulders. The wiry texture of the
fluffy sponge excited her nerves as she smoothed the
foam all over her body.

When she got to her breasts, she moaned as the
rough texture skimmed over her nipples and reminded
her of Keegan MacDonald's slightly calloused hands. She
made another pass imagining his hands there instead of
the loofah, and a wave of need melted her insides.

God, she was mad enough at him right then to
have the best angry sex of her life. When she finished
working out her anger on *him*, he would be *begging* her to
give him a breath. The sexy, snarky, *frustrating* bastard
would be fucked senseless by the time she told him to go
to hell and walked away. The image of that pinched look
on his face at the café came back and she smiled.

In the shower, she could indulge any fantasy she
wanted, so she did. The stress relief of a good orgasm
would help take the edge off her anger, so she didn't
kick him in the nuts when she saw him tonight.

Her hand drifted down between her legs and she
leaned against the wall to finger herself. With each
rotation, waves of heat washed up her body and she
curled her neck to moan in delicious agony. Moisture
flooded her folds and her inner walls pulsed with her
motions. Her eyes drooped closed and his handsome face
appeared.

Those eyes, that hard jaw with the shadow of a
beard she wanted to feel between her thighs. That sexy,
full mouth she knew would taste as spicy as his snarky

words and could give her the pleasure she needed. She bit her bottom lip, pressed against the bundle of nerves harder and her knees went weak as her chin dropped to her chest.

She slid down the wall on a long groan, spread her knees wider and mewled as she brought herself closer to orgasm. "Oh, *yes*—just like that, Boris," she praised, as she rolled the swollen bud between her fingers, before stroking it again.

Her other hand skimmed up her body to her breast and she cupped it, flicked her nipple with her thumb and gasped as her body jerked with intense pleasure. A tingle started low in her abdomen, turned into a rush of sensation that swept up her body to her head to make her feel drunk. Waves of pleasure washed through her body and it shook. A moan gurgled in her throat, then turned into a wail as the waves crashed over her, dragged her under, then tossed her out into an angry sea of delicious release.

A long, shuddering sigh escaped her as she extended her boneless legs and rested her head against the cold, wet tile. She felt much better, but she needed to finish her shower quickly now that the water was running cold. She scrambled to her feet, but froze when a masculine growl echoed off of the tile walls.

Snatching back the plastic curtain, Jules leaned her head out and was mortified to see Keegan MacDonald sitting on the toilet stroking himself through his jeans. Her mouth watered as she sized up the bulge behind his zipper, but she dragged her eyes back to his.

"You could've just invited me in," he said, his eyes sparking green fire.

"If I *needed* you, I would have," she replied, lifting her chin as anger surged up to choke her. The audacity of this man just slayed her. "What in the *hell* are you doing in my apartment, and how did you get in here?"

"I got the code to the door from God while we were on the hotline. Ask and you shall receive. It looks like we're going to be roomies, Natasha."

"When hell freezes over, *Boris*. I'm calling the police," Jules growled, as shock rocked through her. Reaching behind her, she turned off the tap, then without caring she was naked, she stepped out of the tub.

She grabbed a towel from under the sink, then stormed to the living room to get her phone. When she picked it up she wanted to scream.

Brand: *No idea who he's with, but it's very high. Got a call from NSA and you will be sharing your digs with him until the case is over. No other option—just play nice.*

Heat suddenly surrounded her and hot breath fanned her neck, raising the hair there. "I see you got the message from on high?" he said, and his voice enflamed the endorphins swimming in her system to fever pitch, which pissed her off more.

The urge to turn around and kick him in that nice package of his was strong, but she resisted. The last thing she needed to add to her list of problems at the moment was a broken toe. She spun to face him and glare up at him.

"I'll find somewhere else to stay," she grated, her voice raw. "I'll sleep on the fucking couch at the club if I have to."

"Suit yourself," he replied smoothly, crossing his arms over his chest. "I'll be in the guest room here. Now, it's my turn to shower and since turnabout is fair play, you're invited to watch if you like." With a wide grin, he turned and her eyes burned holes in his broad back.

CHAPTER SEVEN

How damned hot was it to sit there and listen to her make herself come when he knew she was thinking about him? Hotter than anything he'd ever witnessed in his life.

Keegan quickly soaped up his body with her body wash. The heady floral scent filled his senses to mix with snapshots of Jules Lawson's gorgeous, naked body. Intoxicated by both, his hand found his cock and he quickly handled his residual problem created by the show.

His toes curled into the pads of his feet and his body tensed. Endorphins built, then surged through his system, his balls tightened and his breath stopped as his tension poured out of him in hot spurts.

With a deep breath of the humid air, he quickly washed off then stepped out of the tub feeling lighter than he had in months. Rotating his shoulder, he walked to the vanity and bent to pull a towel out of the cabinet. Even his shoulder was feeling better at the moment.

He flexed his fingers, then squeezed the side of his right hand and moved his hand up the nerve to his elbow. He sighed when he found it still as numb as it had been since the accident. Pressure built in his chest and dark clouds filled his head, trying to suck him into that vortex, but he fought it. This was as good as it was ever going to ever get, and he just needed to accept that.

Eighty percent was better than useless. *Just forget about the fucking teams and help your brothers by finding the asshole who is betraying them and putting them in danger. That's how you can have their six now.* With renewed determination, Keegan dressed then walked out of the bathroom with his towel in hand.

"Where's your laundry?" he asked as he strode into the living room, but his voice bounced off the walls of the empty apartment.

So she chose to walk six blocks to the club, instead of taking a ride with him. That would make things a lot easier, he thought, as he walked down the hall and found the washing machine. She'd probably be avoiding him like the plague at work, too.

But would that really make things easier for him?

No, because she knew things that could possibly help him. He was sure she had a suspect short list, having been inside for three months now. Opening the lid, he dropped the towel inside, on top of the other things, added some detergent then started the cycle.

Leaning back against the machine, he crossed his arms. He knew everything she'd told her boss so far, which was basically nothing. She could *have* nothing, but Keegan doubted it. Since she was a new agent on the team, he suspected she was withholding whatever she'd found from her supervisor until she was a hundred percent certain of her facts. In her shoes, he would do the same thing.

As contentious as their relationship was, Keegan doubted without a hammer and chisel she would give up those facts to him, either. He would just have to keep on a full court press until she caved. What that full court press would consist of was the question. How far was he willing to go to get that information from her?

Twenty minutes later, Keegan parked his bike on the side of the bar, took off his jacket and stowed it, then put his helmet on the seat. He caught sight of someone walking down the sidewalk toward the club...no, limping. Jules Lawson was a very hardheaded woman, so it served her right.

Shaking his head, he walked toward the end of the building and met her at the front door to hold it open for her. She shot him a hot look from her mascara-streaked eyes, which peeked from under sweaty bangs that were plastered to her forehead.

She looked like hell warmed over, he thought, but still good enough to eat.

He strode in behind her and blinked several times until his eyes adjusted to the dim interior then sat on his stool to scan the club. Nobody was there yet, except a couple of the regulars from yesterday, who evidently came early to get pole position by the stage.

The door opened again and Candi gave him a finger wave as she strode by on the arm of a guy in dark aviator glasses with a ball cap pulled low over his eyes. His muscular build and arrogant walk said he could be military but his hair was longer. That meant he was either *former* military, or a SEAL who didn't have to abide by the Navy dress code.

If he was a SEAL, at his age, mid-forties, he was

probably a Commander. In seven more years, Keegan could've been the same. He sighed and watched Candi kiss him goodbye before she walked into the dressing room.

Her boyfriend didn't take a seat at a table, he sat in a chair at the stage. The side door opened and a thuggish looking man with a long beard walked in. After Rusty checked his ID, he walked directly to the stage and took a chair beside Candi's boyfriend, where the music would be loudest. Where nobody could overhear anything they had to say. God, he'd love to be a fly on that speaker up there so he could hear what they were talking about when they put their heads close together. He may have found his turd, but he needed more than suspicion.

Keegan would have to snag Candi to ask her boyfriend's name if she came to the bar for a pre-show drink like she had yesterday. That's when he'd introduced himself and grilled her about Jules. If he was lucky, maybe he could hit Rusty up to find out the thug's name too.

As it got closer to eight, though, more and more people filed into the bar and Keegan was too busy checking IDs and sizing up the customers for trouble-making potential to even watch for her. Frank was busy slinging drinks behind the bar, so there wasn't a chance in hell he'd be able to talk to him before closing time.

This working while investigating was seriously slowing him down, but he had to do it or he'd be fired. Then he wouldn't be able to investigate anything. Catch 22. He imagined that's what slowed down Jules, too.

Keegan noticed that Candi's boyfriend left at seven-thirty through the side door, shortly after the thug—and before she took the stage. Something was definitely off. Why would he come inside with her, just to leave before she danced?

Because he was there to meet that thug, not watch her dance.

That moved him to the top of Keegan's suspect list, but he wondered where the guy placed on Jules' list, or if he was even on her radar. Finding that out would require talking to her, and she was going to the serving station on the far side of the bar to avoid him.

You can run, Agent Lawson, but you can't hide because I know just where to find you, and it won't be on that ratty sofa in the dressing room. I napped on it after we ate breakfast and know you won't be brave enough to lay your head down there.

See you at home, Natasha.

CHAPTER EIGHT

"Hey, Candi," Keegan said, as he strode over to her when she walked out the back door of the dressing room at two-thirty. He pasted on a grin. "Is your boyfriend picking you up tonight?"

She looked at him and he couldn't get over how much younger she looked without all the stage makeup she usually wore. He almost felt guilty for hitting on her, because she looked barely eighteen. But a man had to do what he had to do. This woman had information he needed.

"No, Blane said he had to work late tonight, so I'm catching the bus. I'm sorry but I need to hurry or I'll miss it." She walked faster, but he easily kept up with her.

"I could give you a ride home, if you like? We could stop for breakfast," he offered, and she stopped to turn and look at him.

"Are you hitting on me?" she asked, her mouth pursed. "Because, if you are, I have to warn you, Blane might kick your ass. He's a SEAL."

One supposition confirmed. That information made his Spidey senses tingle. Now, he was doubly determined find out everything he could from her about his prime suspect.

"I thought he looked familiar," Keegan said, seizing the opening she'd given him. "I used to be a SEAL too—what's his last name again? I might know him."

She shook her index finger side-to-side and smiled. "If I tell you, I'd have to kill you," she said with a laugh. "He tells me that all the time when I ask him questions about his work."

"Well, since I don't want to die, I won't ask you that again." For a little while anyway. "And I promise all I'm looking for is friendship. I want to feed you breakfast and give you a friendly ride home."

She studied him for a minute, and his shoulders relaxed when she smiled. "I would love that, then. Thank you, Keegan," she said, sliding her hand under his arm. "When I saw that bike of yours, I wanted a ride anyway."

His bike was a chick magnet when it was red—now? He could probably have a different woman on the back every night. For a man who said he was off women, he sure had plenty riding bitch on his bike these days.

"I'll give you a ride anytime you want one, sweetheart," Keegan said, with a wink.

"You're definitely flirting with me," Candi replied, as he dropped her arm.

"Sorry, that's a natural response when I'm around a beautiful woman." Keegan grinned as he handed her his helmet from the seat. He opened his saddlebag and pulled out his jacket to slide it on and watched her watching him.

"Where's your helmet?" she asked, dropping her bag to put on the helmet.

"My head is hard enough to take it," he replied, tapping his skull and she giggled.

Movement at the corner of the building caught his eye and he saw Jules come around the corner carrying her bag. She stopped and stared. Keegan could almost see the steam coming off the top of her blonde head as she stiffened her shoulders, turned, and marched across the parking lot, away from him.

You didn't want to ride with me, remember?

It looked like she'd inspected the sofa in the dressing room and found it as disgusting as he did, because she was heading in the direction of the apartment. Shit, she shouldn't be walking alone in this neighborhood at this time of night.

Worry settled in his chest like a lead weight. Even if they were *unilateral* partners, they were still partners, he thought with a sigh. He should be watching her six.

"Can we skip breakfast, doll? I'll drop you off at the bus station, but I just remembered something I need to do."

Her smile faded and she nodded as she pulled the chin strap on the helmet tight. "That's fine—I wouldn't want Blane to catch wind of it, anyway. He gets kind of mean when he's jealous."

Keegan's insides clenched. *Kind of mean?*

"Does he hit you?" he demanded, his fists curling as anger burned through him.

"No, but he's come close a couple of times, so I don't like to push him," she replied, her voice trembling. "He's just one of those alpha SEAL guys. That's how he deals with everyone."

No, *Keegan* was one of those *alpha* SEAL guys and he knew a lot of them too. They were his brothers. *None*

65

Slow Ride

of them would ever hit a woman or threaten to.

"How long have you dated him, Candi? Why do you continue to date him if he threatens you?" he asked, because he couldn't help himself.

"About six months and he pays for my apartment." She shrugged. "He's good to me most of the time." With a sigh, she unbuckled the helmet and pulled it off to hand it to him. "I think it's better if I walk, but thank you for the offer."

Before he could argue, she picked up her bag and took off across the lot. Keegan watched her for a second, then put on his helmet and straddled the bike. If she wasn't careful, her life could be the price she paid for that apartment with a man like that.

Mind your own business, MacDonald. You can't save people from themselves.

But he wouldn't be talking to her again, because that might put her in danger. Now that he had the dickhead's unusual first name, he felt sure he could get more information on him. Someone at the base had to know him or report to him.

His buddies might even know *Blane* and they would give him the lowdown as long as it wasn't OpSec protected. If they weren't wheels up, maybe he'd go have a beer or lunch with them at the officer's club on Sunday.

Cranking his bike, Keegan squeezed the throttle and zoomed across the lot to go find Jules and follow her to the apartment. The traffic on the main road was light, so he caught up to her quickly at the corner just a block from the club. She'd pressed the crosswalk button and waited, even though the streets were almost deserted, making her a sitting duck.

He stopped at the curb and knew *she* knew he was there, because his new pipes were loud enough to wake the neighborhood as he idled nearby.

"Get on the back, Natasha!" he shouted. Her only response was to fold her arms across her chest and stare at the red stick man on the post. *Fine—be hardheaded.* "You do look like you could use the exercise, so I'll just follow you."

"Go to *hell*!" she shouted, before she stepped off the curb and crossed the street.

Been there and done that for twelve years, sweetheart. Fought the devil and won, so you're not going to win this battle of wills.

Keegan idled through the intersection and coasted along the curb as she walked. Two blocks later, she stopped at the next crosswalk and stabbed the button. She spun and put her hands on her hips to glare at him.

"Go find *Candi*. I'm sure she'll let you sleep at her apartment, since you two are such good *friends* and you're *not* welcome at *mine*." She turned back to stare at the crosswalk sign again.

You sound a little jealous, Agent Lawson.

"Oh, I'm welcome. *God* says so, remember?" he replied, and heard her frustrated growl, even over the throaty engine. Oh, yeah, he was getting to her bad.

The little man on the post turned green and

Keegan followed the little green woman as she stepped off the curb. He idled into the intersection beside her and she stopped to spin and slay him with her eyes.

"You're *really* going to follow me all the way to the apartment?" she shouted, pushing the hair out of her eyes with her wrist.

Keegan nodded his head and smiled.

She rolled her eyes, and a sense of victory surged through him when she strode toward the bike, her face a mask of fury. After pushing her bag behind her, she stomped on the back peg and threw her leg over the seat behind him.

She didn't slide her arms around his waist, though. She sat stiffly behind him—until he squeezed the throttle and she had no choice. He hoped she didn't hear his laugh over the roar of the engine or there would be hell to pay when they got home.

Never play the stubborn game with a SEAL, honey, because you will lose.

CHAPTER NINE

"Where are you going?" Jules asked with a yawn late Sunday morning, as she curled up on the sofa with a cup of coffee wearing black flannel pajama pants and a white tank top. "I was going to cook breakfast for us, but I guess I'll just settle for a Pop Tart."

Now, she was offering to cook him breakfast? He was starting to suspect his unexpected partner was resorting to the same guerilla tactics he'd planned to utilize, if necessary, to get information from *her*. Her tactics were subtler—but *effective*—if that was the case.

Keegan tried not to notice that she wasn't wearing a bra under the tight tank. He failed because her dime-sized nipples, which tipped her perfect size B breasts, were saying good morning to him, and his cock wanted to say good morning right back.

It was a very good thing he was getting out of here, he thought, sliding his belt through the loops on his jeans, which were entirely too tight right now. The cease fire they'd settled into since the other night was really fucking with his mind, and he suspected Natasha knew that.

He might have won the battle of wills, but she was winning the war. She was entirely too passive and amenable now, which made this whole setup suddenly seem entirely too…domestic. Images of eating breakfast with her, then having her for dessert flashed through his mind, and he bit back a growl.

With her snark in remission, Keegan was defenseless.

He wished like hell now he hadn't suggested sharing an apartment with her rather than letting Greg set him up in a hotel—just to spite her—because the joke was on him.

"I'm going to the base to have brunch with a few buddies," Keegan finally replied as he fastened the buckle. *And get my head right.* He attached the chain from his wallet to his belt loop, then forced himself not to look at her as he sat down on the sofa to pull on his boots.

"You see Ari at the bar lately?" he asked, trying to refocus on business. She surprised the hell out of him when she responded.

"Nope, he hasn't been in since last Thursday when you saw him. He usually only comes in once a week, so I'd bet he'll be in this Wednesday or Thursday."

He didn't want to wait that long. Hopefully, he could get some good intel from his buddies at brunch so he could finish this and go back home where he belonged. But just in case he got nothing today, lap-dance-loving Ari was next. But right now, since his sexy roomie was in a talkative mood, he was going to keep her talking.

"Does he ever talk to anyone other than Ruby when he's there? Meet with anyone else in that room?" Keegan asked as he sat up.

"He's sat with a few other men to watch the show, but I'm not sure they were *with* him," she replied.

"Any idea what they talk about when they're in the private room?" he asked, thinking again he might want to ask Greg for some com equipment.

She laughed, and he looked up at her.

"No, but if I did, I wouldn't be telling you, *Boris*." She batted her eyelashes over playful blue eyes as she took another sip of her coffee. "I'm still not even sure we're on the same team, so you'll have to do your own surveillance...unless you want to be more forthcoming."

Yeah, not going to work for the ninth time either, Natasha. Not even with the added ammunition of those big, blue eyes framing the question.

"OpSec—so not happening, babe," Keegan said as he pushed up to his feet.

"What is that, *Boris*?" Her voice brimmed with agitation as she stood too. "Secret Squirrel SEAL code or something?"

The soft-kitten was gone and her claws had come out again, which thrilled him, because Keegan could deal with that wildcat.

"Operational Security, and yes, military protocol. It's on a need to know basis with proper clearance, which you *don't* have." Her growl tickled in his midsection, then zipped down to the end of his dick. Oh yeah, needling still did it for him in a big way, but there wasn't a damned thing he would do about it with her.

"I have *top secret* clearance, asshole!" she shouted, following him to the door.

"But you don't have *special access* clearance." He grabbed the door knob, but her hand covered his and he released it to turn around to face her.

"You said you want to be partners, but I can't be

your partner unless I know who I'm working with—I have to know I can trust you." The kitten was back with hurt in her deep blue eyes. "I *want* to trust you MacDonald, so we can work together and solve this quickly."

Those eyes sucked him right in and he swam there for a minute in her disappointment and confusion. She was right—not knowing who you were working with didn't make for a very good partnership, but it was the hand he was dealt.

"I'll tell you what I can, Lawson. I promise." Keegan sighed and put his hand to her face. "But who I work for is not something I can divulge."

That was in his contract and Keegan knew why. Greg Lambert and his cronies wanted plausible deniability if something went south on an operation.

She took a step closer to lay her hand on his chest and it burned through his t-shirt. Something magnetic flowed between them as her lips came closer and her breath fanned his mouth. A hot tingle raked through him, but Keegan fought the draw.

"Even if I said please and promise not to tell anyone?" she whispered, her eyelids drooping to half mast, which made his cock go full sails ahead.

Those eyes begged him, that mouth tempted him beyond his limits. His hand slid to the base of her neck and he pulled her to mouth to his. Her moan vibrated his tongue as he tasted her flavor. Rich, dark coffee, mixed with peppermint, and her own unique sweetness. It was an erotic combination that immediately set him on fire.

She leaned into the kiss, pushed him back into the door and settled her body into the space between his legs. She opened wider and his tongue fit perfectly into the cradle of her hot mouth as she shoved her hand into his hair to kiss him harder.

Keegan's toes curled in his boots as her heat burned though his jeans and her hips made needy little circles against him, making him harder than he'd ever been in his life. A craving to be inside of her slammed into him and almost brought him to his knees.

This woman did not play fair, he thought, as his hands found her hips. Without breaking the hot kiss, he lifted her up and turned to ram her into the door. His control snapped but he knew he couldn't finish this. He couldn't pay the price she'd ask from him for that pleasure.

Taking over the kiss, he ravaged her mouth, ground his cock into the wet heat between her legs and soaked up the pleasure from each moan and mewl of hers that he swallowed. It cost him a lot to finally pull away, to lower her to her feet and step back on shaky legs to run a hand through his hair.

"What's wrong?" she asked, her face flushed and her eyes molten.

"I've got to go," he said, dragging in ragged breaths. "I won't be back tonight. I'm going to bunk with a friend off base. You have my number if you need me."

Keegan opened the door, rushed out and double-timed it down the steps. Letting himself be used again was not something he was willing to allow—and he knew that is exactly what Jules Lawson had in mind to get information out of him. Having his own intended tactics used against him didn't feel so good.

CHAPTER TEN

"Hey, guys, sorry I'm late," Keegan said as he sat down at the table with his former teammates Loren Wilson, Pete Garrison, and Mike Lawrence. They were a sight for sore eyes, but looked pretty damned worn out at the moment.

"You're always late, MacDaddy, which is why you ran so many extra rucks," Wilson said, as he tore off half a roll and shoved it into his mouth.

"Yeah, and you ran with me for trying to cover my ass," Keegan said as he grabbed a roll too. "That was pretty stupid."

"You trying to boost me over that wall in BUDs so I didn't have to take a surf torture was pretty stupid too." Wilson grinned. "What the fuck were we thinking, signing up for the winter class? We almost fucking froze to death."

"What didn't kill us, just made us stronger. Nothing could stop us by the time we got our Budweisers," Keegan replied. He wished he still had that same drive and belief that he was invincible. His shoulder injury brought him back to reality fast.

Wilson's eyes sobered. "How's the shoulder? You thinking of rejoining? Is that what this is about?" He hitched a thumb over his shoulder. "If so, I have an extra set of BDUs in the truck."

Keegan laughed, but his insides clenched. "No, I'm not coming back, but I wish I could. I miss you guys." And that was the truth. So damned much. These guys were more than his teammates, they were his brothers and best friends.

"Wishing never got anything done," Garrison said with a snort. "Get your flabby ass back on the grinder and get 'er done, instead of sitting on the sofa eating bon bons."

Keegan's hand moved to his stomach and glided down the ripples under his shirt. Even though he wasn't on the teams anymore, he still kept up his PT, so he knew he wasn't flabby.

"The only thing flabby is that muscle between your ears, Gars. Might want to exercise that a little more and lay off the beer."

"Beer is the only thing keeping me sane," he replied, picking up his glass to finish it. He slammed it down on the table and waved to their server. "Wife decided she was better off without me, since we've been gone so much this last year. Bitch has my money to keep her warm now, so she doesn't need me."

His *wife* had slept with almost every sailor on base, if the rumors were true, so *he* was better off without *her*. It had nothing to do with how much he was away. Everyone in their squad knew it, but never said anything because they knew it would only hurt and distract him.

"Do any of you know a CO named Blane?" Keegan asked, after the server set another beer in front of Garrison.

"First or last name?" Lawrence asked, sipping his tea.

"I don't know," Keegan replied, picking up his

menu. "He drives a red Vette, if that helps. I think he is or *was* a SEAL."

"Only SEAL I know who drives a red Vette on base is Joel Craddock, but he's no longer on the teams," Wilson said, shaking his head. "He was a CO but they relieved him of command."

"Why is that?" Keegan asked, as a spark of excitement zipped through him.

"He got caught fucking a junior officer in an equipment shed at a forward base during a mission," Lawrence answered, shaking his head. "They tried to keep it under wraps, but someone leaked it to the wives' club hotline. I heard about it from *my* old lady."

"No shit? Wow, what a dumbass," Keegan said, that spark growing brighter.

"Yeah, he's lucky they let him finish out his time being an errand boy for the base commander. I think he still has twenty-two months or so left for twenty," Wilson said.

"No, he was lucky his wife didn't find out the first time he did it," Garrison added. "If that female officer hadn't dropped the harassment charges when she caught him with someone else, he would've been court martialed and divorced two years ago. He was a moron for pushing his luck."

"Word has it that Vette is the only thing he got from the divorce, because he still owed money on it, poor bastard," Wilson added with a low-pitched whistle. "And *that* is exactly why I will never get married."

77

"Even if you did get married, I doubt you'd be stupid enough to fuck a subordinate in the field *on a mission*—that is just insanity," Keegan said. They all knew very well the dire punishment for fraternization, especially in the field. "So his wife took him to the cleaners?"

"Yep, female judge. She got everything except the car and he has to pay for it and the two kids he no longer sees unsupervised," Lawrence replied. "The abuse allegations could have something to do with that, though."

"How in the hell do you guys know all this?" Keegan asked with a laugh, but that information further solidified he had the right guy.

"Wives' club," Garrison and Lawrence replied in tandem.

"Which is *another* reason I'll never be getting married," Wilson said, with a salute. "I never want to be fodder for that grist mill."

"Are we going to eat? My stomach thinks I slit my throat, and I have that feeling," Lawrence said rubbing the area between his eyes.

"Fuck," Garrison said, shoving his beer aside. "I think that metal plate in your head is picking up signals from Mars, dude. We are *not* going wheels up today. I have plans to stuff my gut, then sit in a fucking Jacuzzi at the gym and soak my balls."

"Jesus, man, just the thought of that makes me not want food now," Lawrence said.

"Nothing can keep you from eating, Lawrence,

not even thinking about Garrison's ball soup," Wilson replied with a laugh.

Lawrence waved at the server and she came over with her pad. Before she finished taking their orders, though, three cell phones when off at the same time. Keegan's did not go off, but he tensed and started to push his chair back as a dose of adrenaline pushed through his veins.

"Sorry, dude," Wilson said as they pushed back their chairs. "Blame Lawrence—it's all his fault," he said, grabbing the last three rolls from the basket on the table.

A black cloud descended over his mood as he watched his teammates hurry out of the officer's club, because he should be with them. When they walked out the door, it felt like they took all the oxygen in the room with them. His chest was so tight, he couldn't breathe.

"Would you like to order anything, sir?" the waitress asked, and Keegan shook his head as he pushed back his chair to stand.

No, what Keegan needed right now was to ride as fast and far as he could away from this place, which was about twenty-eight miles to his favorite board rental shack in Virginia Beach. He pulled out his wallet, handed her a twenty, then walk-ran for the door.

As soon as he could breathe again, he would call the commander and tell him he thought he'd found his traitor. That could only be verified though when he saw him again at the bar next week. Hopefully, he could figure out how to get close enough to him and his friend to do that.

But first, while his buddies were going wheels up to fight tangos, he was going surfing and think about nothing except riding enough waves to get past the new funk he felt coming on.

One step forward and three back.

It looked like his shoulder was the least of his problems at the moment. Maybe it was time he addressed that too, and he would as soon as this operation was over. Something had to give, because he definitely wasn't feeling right.

CHAPTER ELEVEN

Tuesday night, Jules was determined not to even look at Keegan MacDonald, who sat brooding on the stool by the front door. When he walked in fifteen minutes late, that was the first time she'd seen him since Sunday. That fact made his position clear on how he felt about the kiss that had almost melted her into the door before he left the apartment. Totally unaffected and embarrassed maybe, that she'd initiated it.

He couldn't be any more mortified than she was that she had taken that first step. He wouldn't have to worry about her doing that again, though. From here on out, his lips were off limits—no matter what her body wanted or her mind conjured as to his wanting the same thing. She had totally misread his signals and paid the stinging price of rejection.

There would be no more softening toward him, or thinking he had loosened up with her. He could tease, flirt, and kid with her all he wanted, but she wasn't falling for his games again. She'd thought about it all weekend, and figured out that's what he was doing—coming on to her to get information. Why else would he have run off like a scalded ape when she turned up the heat and accepted what he was offering?

As for a partnership between them? There wouldn't be any. He could do his own thing, and she would do hers. If she was lucky, he'd continue to shack up with his *buddy*, so she wouldn't have to see him outside of the bar.

I'll tell you what I can, Jules. I promise. Yeah, right. Is that why you rushed right back to tell me what you found out from your buddies at brunch?

If she wanted a permanent spot on the counter-terrorism team, Jules needed to get on the ball or MacDonald would beat her to the arrest. It was on like Donkey Kong now, so he'd better put on his track shoes *and* his thinking cap.

Another conclusion she'd come to, since she'd been able to think while he was gone, was that whoever sent him here had done so because she'd given nothing to Brand so far. They were tired of waiting. His comments at breakfast about her being on the case three months and finding nothing told her that.

With a case like this, which could endanger more military men overseas, the brass would want the traitor found quickly. She wanted that too, and if she hadn't been alone there and slinging drinks while she was trying to investigate, she'd probably have found the leaker by now.

But the military didn't care about excuses, or that she wanted to verify her facts before she presented them. The military wanted answers, so they sent in MacDonald whether Brand or she liked it or not.

MacDonald wasn't her friend—he was *her* enemy—one who could totally destroy what she'd worked for during the last seven years. If he made an arrest before she did, Jules would be headed right back to the white-collar crime task force. She was not going to let that happen. White collar criminals had not killed her parents and by osmosis, her brother.

With a huffed breath, she loaded the drinks Frank handed her onto her tray and turned to go deliver them. Her face planted in the center of a man's chest and she barely saved her tray when she bounced back.

"I need you to do me a favor," MacDonald said, his hands holding her shoulders.

"Why in the hell would you think I'd help you with anything?" she asked with a snort. "Help *yourself*, buddy—I have work to do." She tried to step back, but he held her tighter and leaned closer to her ear.

"I need you to find out what Candi's boyfriend and that guy with him are talking about, because I can't do that." His hot breath scorched the shell of her ear and she tried to suppress her shiver but failed.

Okay, so *Blane* must be on *his* suspect list, she thought.

Why in the hell wasn't he on hers, too? What did MacDonald know that she didn't? Blane seemed harmless when he came in here to drop Candi off—and so did the guy who always came in to talk to him. She never even thought about adding him to her list.

"I'm not doing it unless you tell me *everything* you know about him. If you want that information, we'll trade for it when we get off."

"*Fine*—" he hissed, standing to run a hand through his hair. "Just find out what they're talking about before his partner leaves. It's important."

His partner? Yeah, Blane was definitely on SEAL Boy's radar. That made her feel like the FNG that she was. Give her a white-collar criminal and she could run him to ground in a heartbeat. This was a whole new arena for her, but she was determined to be successful.

Jules went back to the bar to grab a towel, then stopped and dropped off the drinks on her way to the stage. Blane and his friend were sitting at the far end, so she had to discreetly work her way over there, wiping tables. If she didn't hurry, the stage seats would be filled so she wouldn't be able to casually wipe down the bar there. She worked her way table by table to within hearing range, then set about scrubbing a spot on the closest one.

Blane slid his hand across the space between them and lifted his hand. Her heart stopped when she saw a yellow USB drive, which the other man quickly palmed and put into his pants pocket.

"Drop off the same?" Blane asked.

"Yes, it's in the locker. Khal says this better be more than last time."

"Oh, it's more. Last time was a fluke. I almost got busted, so I didn't get everything," Blane replied, then cleared his throat and leaned closer to the man. "Remember Leap Frog."

"Got it—Leap Frog. Later." The man pushed back his stool and stood. Jules quickly swiped her rag over the table, put it on the tray then scurried away.

God, she wished she had her phone with her, because she'd have gotten a photo of the guy with Blane.

He had on a knit beanie cap, so she didn't get a great look at him. Only the three-inch scar on his left cheek above his scraggly beard stood out in his olive complexion.

Jules didn't head toward Keegan, because she was worried she'd be seen. She stopped and wiped several more tables and took a few drink orders on her way back to the bar. When she stopped at the serving window, he stepped up beside her and waited while she rattled the orders off to Frank.

"Flash drive, locker somewhere and Leap Frog," she said, under her breath.

"Thanks. I'm not feeling well, so I'm going to the apartment," he said, and then leaned over the serving window. "Frank, I need to leave. Montezuma's Revenge. Ate some bad Mexican food last night." Keegan added a moan, and puffed out his cheeks.

Jules bit back a laugh as she loaded the first drink Frank handed her on her tray. The man had better hope he was a good secret agent, because his acting skills left a lot to be desired.

"Well, shit—what am I supposed to do for a bouncer now?" Frank asked, his face flushed. "I should've never fired Trace." He jerked the towel from his shoulder and dried off a glass, before filling it with the soda hose. "If you're not back here tomorrow, you're fired. And don't be late—don't think I didn't notice."

"Yes, sir," Keegan said, and nudged her with his elbow as he hurried toward the side door. Jules knew why. He was going to follow Blane when he left, and she wished she could go with him. All she knew was he better be at home tonight so he could fulfill his promise to her or there would be hell to pay.

Jules watched him leave and turned to make the rounds at the new tables, but stopped when she saw Ari walk in the front door with a man she'd never seen before. The music cued the first dancer, the lights dimmed and she lost him. She would just about bet he was going to find Ruby in the changing room.

She turned and walked back to the bar. "I'm going to deliver this drink, then I need to go to the restroom, Frankie. Have Delores cover my tables for a few minutes."

He grumbled something, but Jules didn't wait around to figure out what he said. She set her tray down and headed backstage. Maybe Boris didn't know everything, she thought, with excitement buzzing through her as she worked her way through the crowd. *Her* suspect Ari was here with someone new, on a Tuesday, which was out of the norm for him.

Jules had a feeling something was about to break loose and she was going to find out what that was. Maybe by the time MacDonald got home from his wild goose chase, he would be the one who was beat to the punch on this investigation.

CHAPTER TWELVE

By three a.m. Keegan was more than ready to find a bed and lay his head down, but he was in the back lot at the bar waiting to give Jules a ride to the apartment. Since the traitorous leaker and his partner were now both in federal custody, he had no idea *why* he came back to give her a ride, because except for the indictment and his testimony, the case was over. He could go back to Virginia Beach tonight, if he wanted to, and he did.

Keegan was kidding himself, though. He knew exactly why he was here instead of heading home. He knew Jules would be upset when her boss told her tomorrow the case was resolved, so he wanted to be the one to tell her tonight. He also wanted to thank her and say goodbye, because he might never see her again after this.

His heart took a dive to his stomach, but he forced it right back where it belonged. This was business, and that feeling had no place in the mix.

The information his unexpected partner gathered had been critical to the success he had tonight and he made sure the arresting FBI agents and the Commander knew that. With her help, he'd been able to find the thug at the bus stop, catch up with the red corvette at the nearest bus station, where he felt sure the *locker* was located, and nail Joel Craddock with his payoff in hand. Operation Leap Frog, and the SEALs who were being deployed overseas for that critical mission, were now safe, thanks to her.

The bus provided a good description of the thug, turned radical sympathizer, and his drop off point. When he related that information to the FBI agents who arrested Craddock, Keegan was so pissed by their response, he had to leave the station or throat punch them.

They knew exactly who the thug was and where to find him, because he had been on their watchlist for *two years*. If they had acted instead of sitting on their thumbs and watching him, this whole situation might have been averted and his brothers' lives saved.

Keegan's eyes drifted lower, his body relaxed and he caught his chin just before it hit his chest. Jules better hurry up, because he might just fall asleep on his bike. He glanced at his watch and it was oh-three-thirty. Twenty-one hours since he'd had shut-eye.

The back door of the bar opened and Keegan reached up to unsnap his chin strap so he could give her his helmet, but a man came out, butt first. The door bounced as he fought to drag something outside. The hair on the back of Keegan's neck stood at attention and he bent to pull his pistol from his boot holster.

Jules' blonde head suddenly appeared between two men and she fought like a wildcat. One of them grabbed her hair and they managed to drag her across the lot. Adrenaline made him dizzy as he flew off of his bike, and glanced around for cover, but there was none. His only cover would be going down the row, behind the parked cars.

Crouching low, he ran across the lot watching which direction they went. They stopped at the tenth car and he did, too. Peering around the end of the car, he watched as they opened the back door of an SUV. He waited until both men were visible, then leaned around the end of the car to train his weapon on the forehead of the one who held Jules.

"Let her go, *now*," he growled and both men's bodies jerked. With a moan, Jules took off running toward him and they reached inside their coats. "Don't go there, or I promise you'll be dead before you have it in your hands."

The men froze, Jules ran behind him and Keegan had no idea how they'd get from behind this car to his bike without a bullet in their backs.

"Give me your pistol and go get the bike," Jules said, breathing hard as she crouched behind him. *Give her his pistol? Was she out of her freaking mind?*

"I don't think so, Natasha," he replied, his mind grasping for an alternative.

"I set a class record for the combined shooting course at Quantico," she informed, with a frustrated sigh. "Just give me the damned weapon and get the bike!"

Keegan turned his head to look at her, which was a mistake. A bullet pinged into the side of the metal car, and he was thankful he'd chosen an older model to hide behind or Jules might be dead. He swung back toward the SUV and fired twice, but his only target was one of the tango's legs before the door shut. The yelp told him he'd probably hit the driver, but the other guy was already inside the vehicle.

His eyes streaked to the license plate but he couldn't get the last three digits from the dented metal. The engine revved, sending exhaust plumes to choke him, but he managed to pop off a round into the back tire on the driver's side before the SUV fishtailed across the lot.

The tire shredded as they headed for the exit. *That was dumb, MacDonald. You wanted them to get away, not stop in the freaking lot.* He breathed again when they didn't let that stop them from pulling out onto the road on the rim.

"Let's get out of here," he said, as he took off running toward the bike.

Jules, surprisingly, kept up with him and was there to climb on back after he straddled the bike. Instead of turning toward the apartment, because he had no idea if the tangos knew where she lived, he headed for Virginia Beach.

She hugged his waist tight, plastered her body to his back and Keegan pushed the bike for everything it had. He glanced in the mirror every five minutes to make sure the SUV wasn't on their tail. Twenty minutes later, he finally relaxed and put his tired brain on autopilot to guide them to the shop.

When he stopped the bike in the back lot, his legs felt like electrified noodles as he waited for her to dismount. He turned off the engine and pushed the bike onto the stand but waited until he was sure they'd support him. Staggering to the trailer steps, he opened the door and went inside and Jules followed, shutting the door behind her.

"Nice digs, Boris," she said with a derisive snort. "They must not pay SEALs very well because they spend it all on training."

"God pays better than the military, but this suits me fine," he growled, plopping down at the small table which converted to his bed. "If you don't like it, leave."

"I didn't mean it that way. It's *cozy*, but not what I expected," she said with a grin.

"Just give me the short version of why those men were trying stuff you in that Range Rover and don't give me any bullshit."

"Tell me what happened with Blane first," she countered, dropping her bag on the opposite bench.

"He's in jail and so is his contact. That's all I'm saying for now. Tell me why you almost died tonight, since the investigation is over."

"*Yours* might be over but mine has just begun," she replied smugly, as she sat on the bench across from him. "I overheard Ari and Ruby with a man I'd never seen before in the private room tonight. Something bigger is going on."

"How did you manage that?" Keegan asked, frowning. *Was* more going on? Did he miss something because his focus was on Blane?

"I hid in a broom closet that I found behind the private room. There's a peephole in the corner, which I'm sure is not accidental. If I hadn't been overheard calling my boss to fill him in, I wouldn't have been in trouble."

"You called him from the *broom* closet?! If you could hear them, they could hear you too!" Keegan shouted, because that was just about the most bonehead move he'd ever heard.

"Of *course* not. I had to get my phone from my locker and *Ruby* overheard me in the shower talking to him," Jules corrected angrily.

"You should've waited until you were somewhere secure to call," Keegan replied.

"I couldn't. They mentioned a ship in Baltimore leaving Friday morning," she said, shaking her head. "You know how slow the government works. I wanted to make sure I had backup, but my damned boss blew me off. He may live to regret that."

"What, exactly, did you overhear?" Keegan asked, trying not to side with her boss. Was she just trying to save face by creating a situation where none existed?

She dragged her eyes to her hand and thrummed her fingers on the table. "They talked about a big gesture that would impress everyone on the east coast. The guy who met with them tonight, Abdel, is obviously a leader of some kind. They were very deferential to him and I got freaked out when they ended the meeting with *Allah Akbar.*" She sighed, and met his eyes again. "I probably jumped the gun calling Brand, but I thought it was better to be safe than sorry. There were signs before 9-11 but nobody took action—I wasn't going to be one of those people because I know the cost."

"Well, *Brand* could be pissed that he had egg on his face because of me. I'm sure he got a call from on high as soon as the arrests were made." The name she mentioned soaked into Keegan's exhausted brain and a shot of adrenaline woke him up fast. "Abdel *Nour?*" he asked, his blood freezing in his veins.

Fuck, while he'd been off chasing a squirrel, had Godzilla gone into that strip club tonight?

"I don't know—they just called him Abdel a couple of times and Imam once. Why?" she asked, her brows crashing together.

"Abdel Nour is an Iranian Al Qaeda leader, an Imam, and number eight on the government's top ten most wanted terrorist list." Keegan pulled out his phone and found his most recent list. He opened the photo for Nour and held it out to her. "Is this who you saw?"

She took the phone and studied it for a long minute, while he ground his teeth. When she handed it back to him, she met his eyes.

"It looks like him, but in that photo he's wearing robes, a turban, and has a beard, so I'm not sure. This man was clean shaven and looked like a regular American businessman last night. Polo shirt and khakis."

Keegan didn't want to ask, because his eyes felt like they were lined with sandpaper right then and this wasn't in his mission orders, but knew he had to find out. Especially if it was Godzilla they were talking about.

"What did they say exactly? What ship were they talking about?" he asked.

93

"He will be on the Radiant Sun to pay for the shipment and their friends will be escorting the package back to Baltimore for the party at the end of next week," she replied.

"How do you know they were talking about a terrorist event?" he asked, because he still wasn't convinced. Her information was so thin, he wondered why in the heck *she* thought that.

"I don't, but if I don't at least check it out, considering what I overheard, if something happens, I will never be able to live with knowing I could've prevented it."

"You seem very determined for a woman with very little evidence to suggest your suspicion has merit," Keegan said, scrubbing hand over his face.

"I wish someone had taken that precaution without black and white evidence before 9-11, because my parents and brother might still be alive. I'm going to Baltimore with or without you. I know *your* case is over, so I'll just rent a car if you can give me a ride to the rental agency when the sun comes up."

Keegan's heart crashed to the pit of his stomach as he watched her eyes tear up and his burned, too. God, he couldn't imagine what she must've gone through. She had to have been very young when her parents died. He wanted to find out more about it from her, but now was not the time.

That explained why she was so determined to follow up on this wild goose chase, and why he was going to help her settle her mind.

"No, I'm not letting you go alone, but we both need some rest."

Because wild goose chases took energy which he didn't have at the moment. If she was right, though, Godzilla hunting would take even more effort.

CHAPTER THIRTEEN

Jules stared at Keegan MacDonald's handsome face, stunned, but relieved that he was going to help her. The situation at the bar had been a close call. If he hadn't shown up to help her when he did, she wasn't entirely sure she would be alive right now.

She knew, without his help she could very well find herself in the same position if she went on this fishing expedition alone too. Despite what she said about not softening toward him, she felt like a marshmallow inside at the moment.

Even though he was no longer a SEAL, this man was a hero right down to his core, which was sexy as hell. The fact he was helping her with blind faith in her upped the hero factor. Right then Jules even forgave him for stealing her arrest, because she knew he did it with a good heart, not to spite her.

"Thank you for showing up tonight, and for agreeing to help me," she said, her voice not entirely steady as emotion swirled inside her body.

Why this particular situation was so important to her, she didn't know. There had been plenty of terrorist *situations* since she joined the FBI. It could be because this was the first since she'd been on the counter-terrorism unit, where she could possibly do something.

If what her gut was telling her was right, this could be her chance to help those people who would be targets, instead of watching them die on television like she had her parents.

But going out on this limb could mean you lose your job

with the agency, too. If it didn't pan out, or turned into a goat fuck, the odds were Brand would fire her. As long as she kept her cool, and didn't do anything stupid, it should be fine.

Jules would take that chance, because this was too important not to.

To lower those odds, though, she would do this on her own time, with her own money. She had time accrued so beginning tomorrow, she'd take emergency leave. Should it turn out she was off base here, she'd never tell a soul, but at least she could sleep at night. Well, she could when the nightmares didn't keep her awake.

Keegan MacDonald was her insurance she *wouldn't* do anything stupid. He was a trained Navy SEAL, and she had confidence he knew what he was doing.

God had hired him, right?

"You're welcome, but we need to get to bed now. It's going to be tight in here, but we'll make it work. Stand up," he said, sliding out of the booth.

Jules grabbed her bag and stood, then watched while he removed the table and pole to slide out a partition before he arranged the cushions over it to make a twin bed. *Tight?* She'd have to be sleeping on top of him for both of them to fit.

A shiver racked her as the erotic kiss at the apartment replayed in her head. She definitely wouldn't mind sleeping on top of that hard body, but doubted that's what he had in mind.

He reached above the bed to open a cabinet and

pulled down sheets, a blanket and pillows, then slammed it shut. Before she could blink, he had the bed made and was pulling off his t-shirt. Her mouth watered as her eyes ticked down the middle of his perfect abs to the waistband of his jeans.

"How'd you get that scar?" her mouth asked, without her brain's permission. The three-inch long puckered, pink scar near his left shoulder was the only imperfection on his delicious torso, and stood out in stark contrast to his otherwise tanned body.

"That is my permanent reminder not to let a woman distract me on a mission," he replied, tossing his shirt aside.

Not what she asked, but she wasn't going to press him. She did, however, wonder what the woman who was on his mind when he was injured was like. Jules imagined she'd have to be pretty spectacular for this very focused man to be distracted.

Their kiss certainly hadn't distracted him more than a minute or two, and he hadn't mentioned it since then, or explained why he'd walked out. It obviously hadn't affected him as much as it had her.

He unbuckled his belt, removed his jeans, then laid on the bed with his back flush to the wall. Jules took off her shoes and jeans, and sat on the edge of the bed, where she imagined she'd be sleeping too. But when she stretched out, he surprised her by snaking his arm around her waist to pull her back into his body. They fit together like two pieces of a puzzle, she thought, as her body suctioned to his and his heat soaked into her back.

With a deep sigh, he nuzzled his chin into her hair, then dropped a kiss on the top of her head. Jules sighed, and without permission, laced her fingers with his. Her body went limp and she drifted off to sleep feeling safer than she had in fifteen years.

***

Keegan woke up in a sweat with his right arm completely numb. He freaked out when he tried to move, but it was trapped. He looked down and saw blonde hair sticking out from under his blanket and shook the woman plastered to his body.

"Ceece? You're lying on my arm, babe," he mumbled, his brain in a fog as he shifted her weight on top of him.

Her heat settled onto his morning erection, her face nuzzled into his chest and her hips swayed against his. Keegan groaned as a wave of need swept through him. God, he loved when she did that, because he knew where it usually led. Sleepy, relaxed morning sex was just about his favorite kind.

His hands glided down her curves to her ass and he held her hips tighter against him. She gasped, her lips dragged over his skin and her moan set his nerve endings on fire. He bucked under her to remove his underwear then hooked his thumbs in the waistband of her panties to shove them down to her thighs. She took over and worked them down her legs until she kicked them over the edge of the bed.

99

Her wet heat scalded him as she spread her knees wider to lazily stroke him with her body. She scooted higher, and like a divining rod, the head of his cock found her slick opening. In a dream-like trance, he held her hips to piston himself up into her heat with a sleepy growl.

"Mmm…*ohhh*," she murmured like she'd just tasted the most delicious thing on earth.

The sound made him harder, and her pushing down to take more of him dragged a groan from his lips. Her inner walls pulsed around him, inviting him deeper inside and Keegan held her to drive up into her body.

"God, Cecelia—you feel fucking in*credible*, baby," he growled as a tremor rocked him.

A tremor shook her too, as he skimmed his hands up her silky body to stroke the sides of her breasts, but then she tensed. When the woman whose body his cock was buried in lifted to turn her head and look at him with angry, hurt eyes, he knew why. Shock rocked him, and his mouth flapped, but nothing came out.

"Oh, *shit*—I'm sorry," he groaned, shoving a hand through his hair as she slid her body off him to stand beside the bed and glare down at him.

"Yeah, next time you start something, know who you're with, asshole. I won't be a proxy for your fantasies of another woman," Jules said, bending to snatch up her panties.

With a growl, Keegan vaulted up on the bed to grab her and pull her to him. She fought him like a leashed cat until he rolled her on the other side of him, against the wall. Her eyes ripped him into tiny shreds and he couldn't blame her for being angry, because he was disgusted with himself too.

"I'm sorry, *Jules*—so fucking sorry," he said, knowing how insulted she had to be.

"Who is Cecelia?" she asked angrily. "Is she the woman who distracted you on the mission where you got hurt?"

Keegan laid on his back with a groan and his body tensed as the memory of the firefight with rebels at the Syrian border replayed in his mind. Of loading that shell into the launcher on his rifle, of pulling the trigger and seeing the flash then feeling the hot knife of pain that sliced through his shoulder as the rifle bucked from his hands. The mission recap said equipment failure, but Keegan knew he would've noticed a problem if he'd have been paying attention.

Who was Cecelia? "She was my best friend and the worst mistake of my life. An Army captain who was stationed at Ft. Story," he replied, finally putting the correct label on their relationship. "She was beautiful, smart, easy to talk to, and in love with another man, while allowing me to fall in love with her."

Why did finally saying that make him feel lighter inside? Admitting that it wasn't all his fault? Actually having someone to admit that *to* was a relief.

If Cee Cee had just been honest with him up front about Cade Winters, Keegan wouldn't have let that happen. He probably would have kept the benefits out of their relationship. And he certainly wouldn't have gone to Texas to have his heart blindly stomped on by her rejection.

What he felt was used, and it burned. That fact just further fucked up his head. If that wasn't the case he would not have just made the grave mistake he had with this woman, who he just realized looked and acted a lot like his ex-lover.

"That had to be tough," Jules said her voice softening, but her body still rigid beside him.

"You have no idea. I kept a good face on it as long as I could, but almost broke her future husband's nose in a game of full-contact basketball before I left Texas."

After a minute, she put her hand on his chest. "I'll give you a pass this time MacDonald, but don't let it happen again," Jules said, her tone firm but sympathetic. "Things happen for a reason and that relationship evidently wasn't meant to be. I've been in a couple of those hopeless relationships myself, because I am a shit magnet where men are concerned." She laughed, but it wasn't humorous. "You're a prime example."

Keegan's insides untwisted a little, but he was insulted, too. He turned his head to look at her. It was time for honesty with her and a warning. "You'd better steer clear of me then, Natasha, because a worthless piece of shit is *exactly* what I feel like these days."

Voicing that sentiment loosened the tight band around his midsection a little more, but even as the words fell from his mouth, his eyes zoned in on her lips and his body went rock-hard remembering how damned good she tasted, how intense that kiss had been. Jules Lawson had been totally plugged into the kiss—into *him*—when she kissed him. That is how a woman kissed a man she was interested in, something he realized then Cecelia had never done.

"*No*, you're *not* a piece of shit, Keegan MacDonald, and do not *ever* say that again!" she said, her voice forceful enough to draw his eyes away from her mouth. The intensity in her gaze surprised him. "You are a *hero* who's been hurt in more ways than one, so give yourself a break and time to heal."

Jules punctuated her words with a kiss on his pec and the sensation of her hot mouth on his skin skittered down his body. His breath came out in a rush when she kissed the scar on his shoulder, before kissing the base of his neck. She kissed her way up his throat, across his cheek to the corner of his mouth and his lips buzzed. When she raised up a little, her eyes met his and her breath fanned his mouth.

"Who are you kissing, Keegan MacDonald?" she whispered, her beautiful blue eyes boring into his.

"I'm kissing you, Jules Lawson," he replied, swallowing hard as he was catapulted out of the past and into the present.

She smiled as her mouth moved toward his. When their lips fused, the dam holding back his emotions broke. A rush of vibrant energy surged up to his head to make him dizzy and he felt like his battered soul was being sucked into her body and cleansed.

Keegan let the connection take hold this time, basked in it, instead of running. He shoved his hand into her hair to hold her closer and kiss her deeper. And she kissed him back like he was the only man on earth.

CHAPTER FOURTEEN

Jules could not believe she was about to have sex with another fixer-upper. That hurt and hopeless look in his gray eyes, the same look she'd seen in her brother's, made her powerless not to try to make it go away. She knew the dire consequences of not trying to help.

Are you crazy? You're doing it again, Jules—stop it. Now!

But she didn't want to. This was different from those other mistakes. This man *wasn't* a fixer upper—he really *was* a badass hero and worth the risk, she thought, finding his tongue to tangle it with hers. He might have issues, but Keegan MacDonald had stepped up to help her without a second thought, and she was very sure that was his standard mode of operation.

That thought eased her mind a little as she heartily participated in the second sexiest kiss of her life with a man who'd called her by another woman's name, after he accidentally put his penis inside of her while he was half asleep. She'd like to meet the woman who'd treated him so shabbily and have a few words with her, but right now all she wanted to do was completely wipe her from his mind.

Jules wanted him to remember this moment—to replace that woman in his mind with sex so hot he'd never think about her again. From now on, he'd know who his cock was inside. His body shook, and he tore his mouth away from hers.

"Condom," he said, his voice raw as he reached over the edge of the bed. He found his jeans, then yanked his wallet out of the pocket. She sat up as he flipped through it and smiled when he held up a shiny gold packet like a trophy.

"Is it lubricated?" she asked, as she took it from his hand.

"I don't think so," he replied, his eyes darkening as he watched her tear open the packet with her teeth.

"Let me fix that, then." She winked as she removed the latex ring from the foil to place it between her lips.

His eyes widened, his breathing stopped, and his body tensed as she scooted down his body to his knees. She sat upright and let her eyes take a tour of his incredible body then followed the muscular ridge near his hips which formed an arrow to her destination. She rubbed her palm along his hot, silky, and very rigid length and he moaned as if she were torturing him. When she fisted his thick erection, his hand on her arm stopped her.

"Take your shirt off, Jules," he commanded, his nostrils flaring with each indrawn breath.

She dropped the condom into her hand, then pulled her shirt over her head and unfastened her bra to slide it down her arms. His heated eyes scorched her breasts and her nipples puckered as she tossed it on the floor.

"So beautiful…perfect," he whispered hotly as his eyes fixed on her breasts and he reached up to touch her.

"Let me get you suited up first, Boris." Jules waggled her eyebrows and pushed his hands aside to

106

place the rubber ring between her lips again.

She wrapped her hand around his cock once more and he raised up to watch her with blazing eyes. The hot hiss of breath he released when her lips touched the head of his cock danced along her nerves to drive her onward. Tightening her lips around him, she forced the latex band down over the head of his cock.

"Oh*hh*—that is so*ooo* fucking hot," he growled, shoving a hand into her hair as his thick thighs flexed under her and his knees converged. "So, *so…good*—"

Gently adding her teeth, Jules spread the condom down his shaft as she took more of him into her mouth. When he stretched her mouth wide and pulsed against the back of her throat, she cupped his balls and squeezed as she sucked him hard on the way back up. His fist tightened in her hair, he squirmed and the symphony of ragged breaths and agonized moans excited her.

"You're *killing* me," he growled as his hand tightened in her hair.

By the time she released him with a soft, wet pop it felt like he might pull a fistful from her scalp. Before she could rise up, he yanked her up by her hair and pain sliced through her skull. A thrill zipped down her body when he slammed her back into the wall and pinned her there to devour her mouth. He shoved his hand between them to rake it through her wet folds and she shivered.

Pulling her leg up over his hip, with one forceful thrust he shoved his cock inside her body and Jules moaned at the delicious, burning stretch. A violent tremor shook him and he sighed into her mouth and his ragged breaths became her own as he kissed her harder.

This is why she loved alpha bad boys, she thought—they knew what they wanted and took it. Keegan dominated her, overwhelmed her with his mouth and gripped her thigh with his strong fingers as he pistoned himself into her time and again. But she dragged her mouth away from his, because she had to know.

"Who are you fucking, Keegan?" she asked in a raw whisper and he froze mid-stroke. His muscles tensed and his cock throbbed inside of her.

"Nobody. I'm *making love* to you, Jules Lawson," he growled, his eyes fierce as they met hers, his nostrils flaring. "If that's not okay with you, tell me now, because just *benefits* isn't going to work for me this time."

Emotion shot up to choke her, and she nodded. With a roar, he kissed her again, dug his fingers deeper into her thigh and picked up right where he left off. With each thrust, he drove her into the thin, paneled wall behind her and carried her closer to a blinding release as his cock pounded against her clit with each stroke.

The band of tension twisted tighter inside her squeezing the incredible pleasure higher and higher until it swamped her and her insides quaked. A blinding release shattered her, her body shook in his arms and he held her tight.

When her tremors lessened, he pulled his mouth away to kiss her cheek and his short, ragged breaths seared her left cheek. He lifted her higher, dug his fingers into her flesh and made two more powerful strokes into her body, then went rigid and he roared his release. His heart pounded against hers as he held her there until his body relaxed.

With a shuddering sigh, he laid on his back and pulled her on top of him. She nuzzled her face against his chest and his skin felt like hot, dewy satin under her cheek.

"That was incredible, baby," he whispered and his breath singed her scalp, before he kissed the top of her head.

Someone banged on the trailer door with one hard rap before the door flung back on its hinges. Shock rocked her when Keegan's body jerked and she felt herself falling. He rolled to his knees but fell on top of her, taking her breath.

"Saw your bike parked out here, heard commotion, and thought you might need some help. I ah, see you don't. Sorry, bud," a man said with a snicker.

"We got in late and I didn't want to wake you and tell you we were here. It's all my fault," Keegan said, lifting up on his elbows to take his weight off of her.

Jules craned her neck to look back and see a muscular, gray-haired man with plenty of tats. He looked a lot like Keegan, only about twenty years older and he was grinning from ear-to-ear.

Was that his dad?

"Uh—do you live with your parents?" she asked, blood rushing to her face as she thought maybe she had found another fixer upper.

Nothing like meeting the parents when you weren't wearing a stitch and it was obvious you'd just had sex. Ten seconds earlier and he'd have *really* gotten a greeting.

"I work for my uncle in his bike shop. I own this trailer and he lets me park it back here," Keegan replied, frowning down at her. "You have a problem with that?"

Jules thought about her quaint little house in Franklin that she'd inherited from her grandmother. The one she didn't visit often because of her assignments.

Would she have a house right now at twenty-nine if her grandma hadn't died and left it to her? Probably not, because it really wasn't financially feasible because she was never there. She suspected that might be why Keegan didn't have a permanent home.

"No problem at all," she replied with a smile, bringing her finger up to push up the corner of his mouth. "Your trailer is kind of cozy. Like a tiny house, only the tin can version," she giggled, and he finally smiled.

"Unk—give me a few and we'll be inside," Keegan said, his eyes fixing on her mouth.

"Take your time, Son—I'm just glad..." His uncle cleared his throat. "Glad to see you home." The door slammed and the trailer floor shook under her back.

"If you think this is cozy, you should see the shower," Keegan said, pushing up to smile down at her, his handsome face looking more relaxed than she'd ever seen it. "I have first dibs, so you'll have to wait on the hot water to recharge."

"Very chivalrous of you, Boris," she replied sitting up, her insides feeling light. "Haven't you heard the ladies first rule?"

"Haven't you heard chivalry is dead, babe?" He grinned and the dimple that popped out in his left cheek made her want to lick it. "Equal rights being what they are these days, the hot water is mine."

She laughed as he grabbed his t-shirt and jeans and took a step to open a door in the corner. How in the heck a man as big as he was could squeeze into that small space she didn't know, but the water started running and he banged his way through showering.

The hair on the back of her neck raised and a shiver raced down her spine which had nothing to do with the endorphins swimming in her body. This little unexpected stress-relieving diversion was over.

That feeling of doom was back, and they had work to do. They needed to figure out what that shipment in Baltimore was about fast, before that warning sign turned into a reality.

CHAPTER FIFTEEN

Keegan hung up the phone and sighed. According to the Commander, Abdel Nour had still not been captured, so it *could* have been the Imam at the Lily Pad. There wasn't any intel that he was even in the United States, however, so it could've been anyone in the bar.

Since Jules was unable to identify him by the photo he showed her, as a last ditch effort, he asked Greg Lambert to try and track down a photo of him without the beard and head garb.

Even though last night was supposed to be his last at the bar, he was going back tonight to try to find out what Frank or Rusty knew about the two men. A credit card receipt might yield their last names, at least.

But Jules would not be going with him. Those men tried to kill her last night because of what she'd overheard and would try again if they saw her. That told him there was probably merit to her suspicions. Because he helped her escape last night, they might try to knock him off too, but Keegan wasn't afraid. If they showed up there again tonight, *they* would need to be afraid of him because he had a few lessons to teach them about manhandling a woman.

With a sigh, he walked to the trailer to get his laptop instead of going back into the shop. The only solid piece of information they had was the name of that ship, so he needed to research it before they went off half-cocked to Baltimore Harbor.

Uncle Bob could entertain Jules for a few more minutes, since they hit it off like long lost buds at breakfast. Who knew she was *really* into motorcycles and could talk the talk with Bob? His uncle was certainly impressed with that fact, and with her. He let Keegan know that with several raised eyebrow looks and winks.

He'd just sat down and booted up the laptop when the trailer door opened and Jules came inside smiling. "Your uncle is a riot," she said, sliding into the seat across from him.

"I think he thinks the same about you. Either that, or he's developed some sudden facial tics," Keegan replied with a wink. "I have a feeling if he wasn't married to Aunt Louise, he might ask you to marry him."

"I'd accept," she said quickly, and Keegan looked up to see her grinning.

The sight of that grin did something delicious to his insides. Seeing her happy did too, because now that he knew about her background, he realized she hadn't had a lot of occasions to smile in her life.

"Oh, yeah?" he asked, wanting to keep the playful banter going, so that smile stayed in place. His eyes fell to her mouth and his blood heated as he remembered how good those plush lips felt around his cock.

Next time, she'd be sucking him before she put on the condom. A shiver rocked him, and he squirmed. Something powerful was happening between him and this woman and he needed to pace himself before he let himself be pulled into it.

"Yeah, Bob kind of reminds me of you in a lot of ways," she replied, and her face flushed.

113

"You thought I was an asshole a few days ago," he said with a laugh. "Now you think I'm a hero and awesome like my uncle?" Her opinion of him had certainly done a one-eighty.

Keegan was honored to be lumped into the same category as his uncle, though, because there wasn't a man on earth, even his father, who he respected more than Bob MacDonald.

"I'm a woman, so I'm allowed to change my mind. And you've given me plenty of reason to revise my opinion." Her smile widened, and so did the fire in his body. "You saved my bacon last night, you believed my gut feeling about this situation and, without any evidence, you've agreed to help me stop these terrorists. That is heroism in my book."

"No, it's not—those men tried to kill you last night for a reason," Keegan replied, sobering as he was reminded of why she was here. "They were worried about you repeating what you overheard, which tells me there's something to it. *That's* why I agreed to help you. Well, that and the fact that *my* gut tells me Godzilla might be behind whatever they are planning to do."

"Godzilla?" she repeated frowning, which made him want to lick the cute crinkles between her eyebrows away. He wanted to lick more than that, but they needed to focus right now.

"Abdel Nour—that's our nickname for him on the teams," Keegan replied.

She folded her hands on top of the table and

pinned him with her eyes. "The mere fact you want to find someone on the military's most wanted list, when you're no longer in the military, tells me what kind of man you are—a *hero* who cares more about his country than himself." He loved her stubbornness because it almost rivaled his own.

"I do care about my country first and foremost, but finding Abdel Nour isn't about that for me." Keegan was out of the teams now, but he would always be a SEAL, and as such, was not doing this for the glory. He was doing it because it was the right thing to do.

"Why do you want to find him, then?" she asked, lifting a brow as she sat up and folded her arms over her chest. "This mission doesn't really involve you in that case, because you're a civilian now."

"Because SEALs don't fail and, although I'm a *former* SEAL, I count not finding Abdel when we were looking for him a great failure, which will bother me forever. As long as he's breathing, he's a threat to my brothers who are still on the teams. If I can neutralize that risk to protect them, I will." *And if I can protect you in the process, all the better. Bringing down terrorists is not a one-woman operation.*

Seizing the mile-wide opening to get a few of his burning questions about his new *bi-lateral* partner answered, Keegan closed his laptop and pushed it to the side.

"You've dropped a few hints and I need to know. Why are *you* so hot on this mission? You aren't assigned to it, your boss basically shut you down when you told him what you found, yet here you are investigating something that isn't your business either."

Her eyes welled up again, and she blew out a breath. "Like you, if I can neutralize a possible threat to innocent people and don't, I couldn't live with myself. My parents were killed on 9-11. My dad was a firefighter and my mom worked in tower two. He was in the stairwell trying to get to her when it collapsed."

A tremor that might have registered 8.0 on the Richter scale shook him. His stomach lurched as he reached out to cover her trembling hand with his. Her grief and fear seeped inside of him through her eyes, through her skin.

"I'm *so* damned sorry, honey. That had to be horrific," he said, past the knot of emotion choking him. He wanted to know it all. "Was your older brother a firefighter too?"

"No, John was my *younger* brother who turned to drugs at thirteen to numb the pain and when they stopped working, he killed himself right before his seventeenth birthday."

Rage and grief left him in a roar as he slid out of the seat when the first tear tracked down her face. He pulled her up to her feet and hugged her to his chest, as he fought tears himself. Her body trembled and he squeezed her tighter. When her breath came out on a rush, and she reached up to wipe at her nose, he gripped her shoulders and pushed her back.

"After college, I joined the Navy and became a SEAL because I watched that unfold on TV when I was a kid. It left a lasting impression and those images haunted me. I wanted to kill those evil bastards to make sure that never happened again. Hearing your story makes me so damned glad that I did," Keegan said, admitting something he'd never told anyone else.

He'd never said that out loud, because he imagined that could've been a mark on his psych evaluation, which may have kept him off the teams, and he was determined to get into BUDs. Her emotional baggage was so much more, and the feds knew it from her background check. That probably explained why they wouldn't allow her on the counter-terrorism team.

That baggage could cause her to snap and do something crazy during an operation. Like going rogue to follow this lead alone, which was exactly what she had been planning to do if he hadn't stepped in to help. That proved she wasn't capable of rational thought or calm deliberation where a potential terror threat was concerned.

Her instability could also put *them* in danger on this mission if any of her suppositions came to fruition and they came face to face with Abdel.

Keegan swallowed hard. "Are you sure you want to chase this, baby? I have connections and could call it in to Homeland Security and they could investigate it."

That was the smart thing to do here, and he hoped she agreed. If she didn't, he was not letting her go off alone.

Greg Lambert had certainly perked up when Keegan asked about Abdel Nour and told him about what Jules overheard, but he couldn't authorize him to investigate it, since that was not part of his mission and he had no evidence to support it. If he got evidence, though, Greg wanted to know about it immediately.

"*Yes*, I want to chase this, because this is an immediate threat. The feds could take *months* to follow up and we don't have months," she replied firmly.

"Okay then, let's get to work, Natasha."

Keegan sat back down and pulled his laptop to him. If she was determined to do this, he was determined to make sure she didn't get herself killed.

CHAPTER SIXTEEN

"It's a *cruise* ship? Are you sure?" Jules asked, getting up to lean over his shoulder to look at the screen. Leaning in, she quickly saw he was on the website for Radiant Seas Cruises, an exclusive boutique cruise line. "Do they have any cruises pulling out on Friday?"

"Yes, only one. It's seven days." He clicked open the link to see the full description of the cruise. "It stops in Bermuda, Tortola, and the Dominican Republic."

Inside and balcony cabins showed as sold out, but there were suites available. She couldn't imagine how much *that* would cost. She quickly found out when he shocked her by clicking on the "Book Now" button. Her breath froze in her chest as she covered his hand with hers.

"No, we *can't* do that!" Her heart stopped when she saw the opulent suite, which explained the opulent price tag.

"You only live once, right?" he said with a laugh as he moved through the booking process to choose the *Captain's* suite. "Don't worry about it. I just made a healthy chunk of change by plugging that leak for the government."

"But you just can't," she said, covering her mouth with her hand.

"You do have a passport, right?" he asked, ignoring her.

"Yes, but it's at my house in Franklin," she replied. And other than one trip to Nassau eight years ago when she wanted to try out her new scuba certification, it had never been used.

"We'll go by there before we go to the port on Friday. You'll need to pack anyway."

Jules' head was spinning from the speed he was making these decisions. Cruises took time to plan, but not for him evidently.

She didn't know if she had that much time banked at work to take off a week, no, ten days, with the wait time. And the agency usually required thirty-day notice for leave, unless she had an emergency. If her suspicions were true, this situation definitely qualified.

But was she making the right decision doing this? Was she confident enough in her gut feeling to bet ten thousand dollars of *his* money on it?

"I can't let you spend that kind of money on this operation, Keegan, it's too much. What I overheard *could* be related to a party next week and not a terror event. Hell, they could be picking up a hundred cases of caviar, for all I know."

He turned a disbelieving stare on her. "Don't be flip-flopping on me now, Natasha. You were confident enough before now to chase this lead. What's changed? Are you doubting yourself now? Because self-doubt is not a good trait for an agent to have."

"No, I'm not doubting what I heard or suspect," she replied, her shoulders slumping. "I'm doubting you spending that kind of money for us to go on this ship without knowing who or what we're looking for. Maybe we could just be here when the ship comes back to port? That might be more prudent."

"Too late. We're going and you need to have confidence in my abilities, even if you don't have any in your own. Just stop worrying and get ready for some fun in the sun and waves."

"Waves?" she asked, perking up as a rush of excitement pushed through her. She hadn't surfed since before she went through Quantico. Her beach bum, surfer boyfriend at the time taught her how and she quickly got hooked.

"Yeah, Tortola has some of the best surf spots around and I'm an addict. I've been eyeing those locations for years to keep my sanity while I was deployed. I'm making this a working vacation, and that will be my reward." He finished the reservation by entering a credit card number, and Jules was pretty doggone impressed he had it memorized.

"I haven't hit the waves in forever," she said, and he turned his eyes to her again.

"You surf?" he asked, looking dumbfounded, but pleased.

"Not in a long time, but I love it," she replied and his grin lit up her insides like a flash bang. That smile did things to her. This man did more. Keegan MacDonald was every man she'd ever dated, minus the things that made those men a mistake, with a lot more muscle.

"Then I'll book the shore excursion for two instead of one once we get on board. Here, sit down and fill out your information, so I can finalize this."

He stood and she squeezed around him to sit at the computer. Once she filled out all of her information, she moved the cursor to the "Submit" button and looked up at him. "Are you sure about this?" she asked once more.

"I'm sure," he replied, and that grin reappeared. "More sure than of anything I've done recently. We both deserve this and if we catch a bad guy in the process, even better."

Jules looked back at the screen and her hand shook as she hit submit and the wheel that would take her on a Caribbean adventure started spinning. She really did feel like Natasha from Rocky and Bullwinkle at that moment and Keegan was Boris on steroids.

"Thank you," she said once the confirmation screen appeared.

"You're very welcome," Keegan replied. "Now, I've got to get ready to go to the bar."

Shocked, she spun in the seat to look up at him. "Why would you go back there? Our investigation is over!"

"No, it's just beginning. I need to see if I can get more information on Ari from Frank or Rusty. I at least want his last name, because that will help us figure who and what we're dealing with on this mission."

"*No*—those men saw you last night. If they see you, they'll kill you!" Jules shouted, as she pushed up to her feet.

"Plenty have tried, sweet cheeks, and I'm still standing here. No worries, I'll be fine." Keegan put his fingers under her chin and tipped it up. "I won't let them kill me, because I'm going surfing with you...and *other* things," he murmured, before fitting his mouth to hers for a hot, lingering kiss that curled her toes.

"Then I'm going with you to watch your six," Jules said when he pulled away, her heart pounding and her stomach sick at the thought of him going back into that viper pit alone.

"Nope, you are going to stay here with Uncle Bob, because they *will* kill *you* if you go back in that bar and they're there. Watching *your* six will distract me."

Jules smiled tightly, but her mind whirled. If Keegan MacDonald thought she was going to sit here worrying about him, he had another think coming. They were partners and she was going to make sure he didn't walk into a trap.

She waited until he dressed and left, then went to the shop to talk to Bob. She was sure his ex-military, motorcycle-maniac uncle would have the same problem she did with Keegan going off into danger alone. Bob would help her, and tonight, they would ride—whether Mr. I'm-too-sexy-for-a-bullet SEAL Boy liked it or not.

CHAPTER SEVENTEEN

"You ready to roll, Uncle Bob?" Jules asked, as she rushed into the shop through the back door, her body buzzing with adrenaline.

She stopped beside his bike and pulled the black and hot pink skull cap out of her back pocket to tie it on, while he attached a leather sheath of some kind to the side of the bike. He looked up at her and smiled Keegan's smile, dimple and all. His gray crew-cut hair and neat gray chin-strap beard were the only things that separated him from what his nephew would look like in twenty years.

"Nice makeup, babe. I don't think anyone would recognize you."

"Thanks. I'm getting pretty good at this disguise thing," Jules replied with a laugh.

If she got any heavier with the cat's-eye shaped eye liner and smoky eye, she'd look like she'd been punched in the eyes. The fake lashes Louise gave her took it to another level, so did the red lipstick. But the most badass thing about her ensemble was the black hair pieces on combs that she weaved into Jules' hair. Once she braided it, Jules looked like she had black hair with blonde highlights.

"I have to say, you look damned hot in Louise's leathers. Jeans are a little tight, but there's nothing wrong with that either," Bob said with a whistle. "Better not scuff the leathers, or I'll have to answer to her."

"I'm going to ask her where she got them. I'll probably have to get a second job to pay for them, but I think I need this outfit," Jules replied.

The black fringed chaps and studded, cut-waist jacket made her feel as badass as she needed to feel tonight. So did the 9 mm Colt Bob loaned her, which was tucked away in the waist holster under her tank top.

If anything went down tonight, she and Bob would be prepared to handle it, she thought, as she watched him shove a short shotgun into the sheath then flap the end over it. That weapon was totally illegal, she knew that, but when dealing with terrorists, who cared? She almost hoped that Ari and that guy were at the bar tonight, so they could take them down.

But they wouldn't do anything if they didn't have more evidence.

They were only going there tonight to watch Keegan's back in case those men decided to attack him. Bob said the only way he would go was under those terms. He was taking lead and she was support. Typical male attitude, especially one who was a former Army Ranger. It was a little irritating, but Jules agreed, because she wasn't stupid enough to take a cab there alone.

He stood, then walked to a bench and came back with a flat-black half-shell helmet with sparkly pink writing on the front that said Bob's Bitch. She took it from him and ran her fingers over the writing.

"I'm honored," she said with a wide smile as she put it over her cap and snapped on the chin strap.

"You should be," he said, gruffly. "Louise hasn't let a woman ride bitch with me for twenty-five years. She likes you."

A warm rush of feeling flowed through her. It had been so damned long since she'd had a family, she felt honored that Keegan's aunt and uncle had accepted her so easily. She couldn't get too comfortable with them, though, or too attached.

Even though he said it wasn't what he wanted from her, she and Keegan were just friends with benefits at the moment. There was the potential for more, but she wasn't rushing anything with him. Now wasn't the time for it, anyway.

Bob got on the older, but tricked-out Harley Ultra Glide and cranked the throaty motor. The purr rumbled through her body, lighting up every nerve. She stepped on the back peg, swung her leg over the saddle behind him and smiled as she put her arms around his waist. He walked the bike around then clicked a button to open the bay door.

Excitement surged through her as he juiced the throttle and they sped through the door into the dusk. Forty exhilarating minutes later, he idled up into the parking lot of the Lily Pad and it was packed. She saw Keegan's bike parked in his normal spot by the back door, and pointed Bob around the side building.

He parked in the alley behind the dumpster and she got off and removed her helmet. Bob removed his helmet and put it on the seat, then tugged on a black leather skull cap. After he stowed the shotgun in the saddle bag and locked it, he took her hand.

"Let's do this thing, Nat," he said, grinning down

at her. "Operation Save Dumbass has commenced. Where do we go?"

"We have to go in the side door. Keegan will be at the front." She led him around the building to the door and grabbed the handle. "It's Thursday, so it should be packed tonight. That will give us cover."

Jules opened the door and tensed when she saw Trace sitting on a stool there. The loud crowd and bump and grind music insulted her ears as he gave her a quick once over, then a slower double take.

Bob stepped in between them. "Stop eye-fucking my old lady, kid," he growled, in a tone that raised the hair on the back of her neck. She imagined Trace was shitting his pants right then. If he used that tone on her, she definitely would have been.

"Sorry, dude—she's just—hot. I was appreciating. Welcome to the Lily Pad," he replied, giving Bob a chin nod, trying to pretend he wasn't affected. "Cover is ten each."

Bob pulled out his wallet, which was attached to a chain on his belt loop, and handed Trace a twenty. He put it back in his pocket and grabbed her hand, then without another look at Trace, he pulled her with him into the thick crowd. It swallowed them up, and Jules took over because she knew the way. Even so, it took almost ten minutes for her to weave her way to the back through the mass of bodies.

She looked at the empty stool by the front door and frowned. The hair on her neck raised again, this time alerting her to the fact that something was off. Twisting, she leaned back and tiptoed to put her mouth by Bob's ear.

"Something's wrong. He's not at the door," she said and Bob nodded. Easing back down on her heels, she looked toward the bar and saw Sara, Frank's twenty-year-younger, ex-stripper girlfriend tending bar. Frank was nowhere to be seen. Definitely odd. Glancing at the stage, she saw that the twins were on.

"Let's see if he's up front handling a situation." Gripping Bob's hand tighter, she led him across the bar. By the time they got to the other side, Ruby's music cued and she froze.

The stripper strode out of the shadows in her flowing red cape and a deafening roar filled the building as she danced toward the edge of the stage. She tilted her head, then worked the cape dramatically over the heads of the men lining the bar.

Jules glanced at Bob, and his tongue hung out as much as the men in the crowd. She tugged his hand and his head snapped back to her. He leaned closer. "Sorry, just getting my ten dollars' worth," he said with a grin. "Who do I ask for change?"

"Frank," she replied, tugging him back into the crowd to work her way to the stage. "But he's not at the bar either." He was always at the bar, so that fact alone made her insides clench.

At the far corner of the stage she stopped to scan the row of men by the stage, then moved across the front tables to see if Keegan might be there. He wasn't, so she glanced up at Ruby then casually made her way to the backstage door.

It was the only place he could be, other than Frank's office. She paused before pushing through the door to gnaw her bottom lip. If she went inside the dressing room, she knew someone would recognize her. She hated to send Bob in there alone, but she had no choice. Grabbing his arm, she pulled him into the area where the private rooms were located and where it was ten decibels quieter.

"See if he's in the dressing room. If anyone stops you, tell them you're Trina's boyfriend. She's off tonight, so that will be your ticket out." She walked to the first private room and tiptoed to glance inside the window. Candi was in there giving a private dance to someone. She walked back to Bob and leaned close. "There's a closet behind this room, so check it too. If you don't find him, we'll go to Frank's office."

He nodded and they went back to the dressing room door. Before Bob could go inside, it swooshed open and fear slammed into her when Ari walked out, texting on his phone. Jules quickly turned her back and he strode by without looking at her. He stopped behind the men lining the stage and watched Ruby. When she noticed him, he gave her a finger wave, sliced his index finger across his throat then tossed a thumb over his shoulder. She nodded, then glanced at the dressing room door.

Jules' blood turned cold as Ari breezed past her to go back into the dressing room. He never went in there with Ruby. They always talked in the private room. She spun on her heel to grab Bob's arm.

"Something is wrong!" she said, her heart dropping to her stomach. If they went inside the dressing room, she knew they'd walk right into whatever was going on, so she pulled him back to the side door and rushed him outside.

"What's up?" Bob asked sounding agitated.

"Ari never goes into the dressing room with Ruby. Frank doesn't allow it and he was in there without her. He's part of our investigation and the one who tried to shoot us last night. I have a bad feeling Keegan is in trouble." Jules looked and saw Keegan's bike was still there. "Back door," she said then took off running toward the other end of the building.

When she got to the turn, she stopped in her tracks when she saw Ari's SUV idling by the door. Bob plowed into the back of her, almost shoving her into the open. He grabbed her shoulders and pulled her back.

"What in the *hell* is going on, Jules?!?" he demanded as his fingers dug into the leather jacket.

She didn't have to answer when the back door suddenly opened and two men dragged another man out between them. Her hand shook violently as she reached under her shirt to pull out her pistol. What she was going to do with it, she didn't know at the moment.

"That's Keegan," she said, her voice breaking as

fear like she'd never known made her knees buckle.

"Nah, he'd never let them—" Bob started, but leaned over her shoulder again. "Fuck, that is him!" Before she could stop him, Bob rushed out into the open with a pistol trained on the men. Jules had no choice but to stay there and provide cover from the corner of the building. She crouched and chose Ari as her target.

"Stop right there or I'll put a bullet in both of you before you take your next breath," Bob shouted and the words rang in her head.

The men froze and dropped Keegan's limp body to raise their hands. "Walk toward me *now*," Bob instructed, stopping halfway to the truck. Jules was surprised when they complied. "Now get on your knees and lace your fingers behind your head." After a second, the two men did that as well. "Nat, call the police," he shouted.

Jules, reached into her pocket and pulled out her cell phone to dial 9-1-1. When the operator answered, she told them she needed an ambulance and the police at The Lily Pad. When the woman tried to keep her on the phone, she hung up, because she needed to focus on watching Bob's six, and on whether Keegan was breathing or not. Her stomach knotted, then rolled at the thought he could be dead.

God, please let him be breathing. He's a good man and the world needs him. She needed him.

When he moaned and rolled onto his back, she finally breathed again. Distant sirens blared and her chest expanded enough for her to take a deeper breath. This whole situation was surreal to her. Combined with Ari's actions the other night, this verified she had valid reason to be concerned about what she overheard them talking about.

If they were willing to kill two people over that information, something was definitely going on. They had to get on that ship tomorrow. She hoped that Keegan wasn't hurt too badly for that to happen, or she'd have to go alone.

The door opened again and Jules swung her pistol there as Ruby walked out wearing a short, red robe. She knew Bob couldn't take his eyes off the two men he had on their knees, so she walked around the corner.

"Stop right there, Ruby," she growled, mimicking Bob's tone with the men. It didn't work on the woman, and Jules cursed as she darted back inside the door. She ran to the door and flung it open. When she stepped inside, a flash of gray caught her eye and instinct made her duck. A metal chair slammed into the door right above her head.

Adrenaline made her dizzy as she rolled away and came up to her feet, but Ruby swung the chair again. It connected with her right wrist and pain sliced up her arm. The pistol flew from her hand to skate across the floor and Ruby ran for it. Jules flew to her feet then launched herself toward her and tackled the taller woman.

They landed hard, with her on top and slid across the floor. They stopped with the pistol right beside

Ruby's right shoulder. Heart pounding, Jules reached for it, but Ruby's hand closed around it first. Jules jammed her elbow down into the base of the other woman's neck, then hammered her fist into her wrist.

With a yowl, Ruby released the pistol and Jules grabbed her thumb to twist her arm up behind her back.

"Move and it will give me great pleasure to break your fucking neck, bitch," she growled, pushing her elbow deeper into the curve of Ruby's neck, hoping she'd choke off her breath. She would love to kill her at the moment.

"What the hell is going on here?" Frank mumbled as he staggered around the corner holding the side of his bleeding head. "Where the hell is MacDonald?"

"Outside," Jules replied, hoping like hell Frank wasn't one of the bad guys. If so, she was screwed.

"Is he alive?" Frank asked, groaning as he put his free hand on the bench in front of the lockers before he sat down.

"Yeah, he's alive," she replied, relief making her giddy. The loud sirens outside the back door compounded that feeling. The cavalry had arrived and they would be okay.

The back door burst open and a shiver zipped down her spine as she felt guns pointed between her shoulder blades.

"I'm a federal agent, and this woman is under arrest," Jules said firmly.

"*Federal* agent?!?" Frank shouted, then groaned.

With a sense of accomplishment, Jules put her

knee down and lifted her arm from Ruby's throat as she pushed up to her feet. She pulled Ruby up then turned her over to the two policemen, before she picked up her pistol and went to find out if Keegan was indeed alive.

CHAPTER EIGHTEEN

"I'm not going to the hospital, Jules—just drop it!" Keegan repeated for the fifth time, as he sat on the bumper of the ambulance while the medic applied a bandage to the cut near his temple. He ran his fingers around the edges of the small cut, which bled like he'd been scalped, sending sharp rays of pain through his skull.

"You could have a concussion, buddy. This laceration could probably use a stitch or two as well," the second medic warned.

"I've had worse paper cuts and I have a headache. All they'll tell me to do is stay in bed for a day or two. I don't have a day or two." He would be in the middle of the Atlantic on a ship with possible terrorists in a day or two.

Keegan wished like hell they'd just drop it, because they were *giving* him the headache. If he had a concussion, it wouldn't be his first. Yes, it hurt like hell and he felt dizzy, but tomorrow he would be fine as long as he was on that ship before it sailed.

Things got real tonight.

Something huge *was* going down on that ship and he would be on board to stop it. The fact that Ari followed him into Frank's office with his muscle to pistol whip them solidified that.

Thank God he hadn't brought Jules with him tonight. He was pretty damned pissed she'd talked his uncle into bringing her here. But he was also grateful she went with her gut, because otherwise, he could be dead. And damned if she didn't look smoking hot tonight in those leathers.

Even with a concussion he didn't miss that.

At least he'd gotten Ari's last name before they knocked him unconscious. He needed to call the Commander and put him on notice that Ari Alil Abdulla, number ten on the government's most wanted terrorist list, was locked up at the police station in Norfolk.

That was a very good thing, but he knew if the Commander didn't step in and have the Department of Justice file the *real* charges, Ari would likely lawyer up and be out on bond in a few hours on the assault charge. Then they would never find him again.

"Thank goodness Ruby took a swing at me with that chair. At least she's going downtown tonight too," Jules said, waking him up.

"Yes, and thank goodness she didn't connect with your hard head," he growled pinning her with his eyes and she made him angrier by smiling. "Maybe if she had, though, she'd have knocked some sense into you."

"Did Ari knock some sense into your hard head? Do you now realize you don't have to do everything alone?" she fired back, raising an eyebrow.

Yes, he did, as a matter of fact, because Keegan wasn't getting on that ship with only her tomorrow afternoon. He would have help, if the guys could get a leave chit approved on a quick turn from Lieutenant Bledsoe.

"Where's Uncle Bob?" he asked, hissing as the medic rubbed ointment on the cut.

"He's going home to make reservations for him and Louise to be on the cruise tomorrow too. He said there's no way he's letting two rookies go on this operation alone."

"Fuck me," Keegan growled, closing his eyes as the medic taped on the bandage. After he applied the last tape strip, Keegan got to his feet and his stomach lurched when the ground moved. Jules grabbed his arm to steady him.

"You're riding bitch tonight, Boris, so give me your keys and hop on." Jules laughed when his mouth dropped open. Keegan jerked his arm from her grasp.

"No way am I letting you drive me *anywhere*. Are you nuts?!?" he shouted, then groaned when a lightning bolt sliced through his skull.

"I must be, because we're going to my house tonight so we're ready to roll in the morning. Louise said she's packing your bag, and they will bring it with them to the port. It's only an hour fifteen or so from here." She held out her hand, palm up, and gave him the evil eye with her exotic cat eyes. "You scared to turn over control, SEAL Boy?"

Fuck yes, he was! That was a very expensive bike which he'd just finished retrofitting. And it wouldn't just be turning over control—he'd be putting his *life* in her hands.

"Do you even have your endorsement? Have you ever *driven* a bike before?" he asked, his vision going a bit hazy as his insides clenched.

137

"My sport bike is at home in my garage, so yes, I have my endorsement *and* I've driven a bike. Just not in the last five years or so, because of work."

Keegan stared at her for a moment, trying to get his mind together enough to make a decision, and he finally decided he really wasn't in any shape to operate that motorcycle right now. With a sigh, he shoved his hand into his pocket and his stomach rolled when he dropped his keys into her hand.

Please don't kill us, he prayed. *You only live once, MacDonald.* There were worse ways to die than with his arms wrapped around a badass woman who seemed as custom-made for him as his badass bike. Jules turned and her perfect ass, which was framed by studded leather chaps, grabbed his eyes and didn't let go until they were standing beside the motorcycle.

She put on a helmet, then turned to hand him his. His eyes locked on the pink glitter words marking her as *Bob's Bitch* on the front. A laugh rumbled up from deep inside him and escaped. In addition to the Louise's leathers, she must've borrowed her helmet, too. But she was never wearing that helmet again after tonight.

Because he was buying her a helmet that said *Keegan's Bitch*.

Too much, too fast, bud. You've known her less than two weeks. Then why did it feel like he'd been waiting for her a lifetime?

"Are you going to take your helmet or stand there staring at me all night?" she asked, and he dragged his eyes to hers.

"What if I choose staring?" he asked with a grin, as his eyes dropped to her perfect breasts before taking a slow ride down her S curves to the toes of her boots.

"Then you won't get to sleep in my bed tonight," she replied, and his eyes flew up to hers. "I have a lot of adrenaline to burn off, and you're the man who's going to help me get rid of it."

Concussion? What concussion? Oh. Hell. Yes. He. Was. He'd have to be dead not to take that offer, and then he'd still try.

She shoved the helmet into his gut then turned to throw her leg over the bike. When she cranked it, Keegan smiled as he put on his helmet. He straddled the bike behind her and had no problem wrapping his arms around her waist.

He knew he looked like a fool riding behind her, but he also knew there were plenty of men who would do the same for this privilege. He knew of three men at least, who he would be calling when they got to her house.

Keegan had a feeling he was going to have to fight at least two of them on this cruise, once they met her. The third would have been in the mix too, if he wasn't smarting from his divorce. But they could all get behind *him*, and his uncle could too, because Jules Lawson was *his* bitch.

Thirty minutes into their ride, Keegan finally relaxed and enjoyed the novelty of letting someone else have control. The fresh air cleansed the nasty bar smell from his senses and replaced it with her scent as the rushing wind forced it into his nostrils where his nose was buried near her neck.

If he didn't think she'd wreck, he'd lick the smooth, hot skin, explore her body with his hands since they were free. Instead, he bided his time as his cock got harder and harder, the deeper it settled into the crevice of her ass checks.

Closing his eyes, he pictured his warrior princess in those leather chaps without the jeans underneath. That made his problem worse, but it hurt so good. He was so wrapped up in his fantasies, he didn't realize they'd reached their destination until she stopped the bike in front of a neat little gingerbread farmhouse, which was framed by a copse of trees on a wide lot.

She killed the engine but it still rang in his ears as he got off of the motorcycle and removed his helmet and every ounce of tension left him as he studied the brightly lit wide front porch, which was home to a swing at one end and two rocking chairs at the other.

The house looked like it belonged in a Norman Rockwell painting, or on a postcard, but it was so much in contrast to the woman who lived here, he almost laughed.

"So this is home?" he asked as he placed his helmet on the seat after she got off the bike.

"It was my grandmother's house, but yeah, it's home," she replied, as she set her helmet beside his on the seat.

But now it was hers because her grandmother was dead too.

Compassion slammed into his gut like a fist as he stared down into her glassy eyes. This house represented even more grief that Jules Lawson had lived through in her nearly thirty years on this earth. If it was true that what doesn't kill you makes you stronger, she must be made of steel by now.

She grabbed his hand and dragged him toward the porch where she stopped to pick up a rock beneath a bush. He watched while she twisted it and it opened to reveal a key and removed it before she dropped the gray plastic rock back where she found it. He followed her up onto the porch, waited while she opened the door, then pushed her inside and shut it behind him.

Jules took a step, but he grabbed her arm and spun her toward the door.

"About that adrenaline…" he whispered as he pushed her against the wall, tipped her chin, and up covered her mouth with his.

CHAPTER NINETEEN

Jules' moan sent fire through him as Keegan held her face to kiss her deeper. Her hands pulled at his jacket and without breaking the kiss, he managed to shed it. Jules let her jacket drop to the floor at her feet, then her hands immediately went to the button on his jeans as her hot tongue wrapped around his. She lowered his zipper, turned him to the wall and shoved him back into it to kiss him again.

This woman was his every fantasy come to life as she dragged her mouth from his to push his jeans and underwear down over his hips. Every muscle in his body seized when she dropped to her knees in front of him and took his cock in her hand.

He held his breath as she leaned in and her hot, quick breaths scorched the head of his erection. The wet heat of her mouth touched down on his skin and his knees buckled.

"Oh, *God*," he groaned, his toes curling in his boots. Her fist tightened around him and she looked up at him with those gorgeous cat eyes and a sexy, snarky smile.

"Sorry, your boss isn't here to save you, MacDonald," she said with a laugh. "You're at my mercy tonight."

A tremor rocked him as his eyes fixed on her full, red lips. He didn't want to be saved—he wanted that mouth to take him to his knees and finish him. And it almost did when she focused on her task, pursed her lips then lowered her head.

He hissed as red hot lightning sizzled through him

when the wet heat of her mouth touched the sensitive tip of his engorged cock. She pursed her lips and slowly forced the mushroom-shaped head through the tight ring of her pursed lips and he groaned as she took her slow, sweet time squeezing him into her mouth.

A ragged sigh escaped him when he was finally inside the hot cavern, but his relief was short lived. She curled her tongue around him, sucked him harder as she pumped her hand and took more of him into her mouth. Keegan grabbed the sides of her head and roared as he rammed his head back into the wall and light flashed behind his eyelids.

Pain exploded inside his skull to mix with unbelievable pleasure when she sucked him deeper and her tongue dragged the underside of his length. Two more hard sucks and he was throbbing at the back of her fucking throat. Barely breathing, he fought to stop the orgasm that was so close he could taste it.

She moaned deep in her throat, the vibrations traveled through his balls and they tightened. The pressure of her lips lessened, but her teeth raked his skin as she eased him back out of her mouth. It was more than Keegan could bear. With a growl, he pushed her mouth away just as cum rushed up his cock in a hot wave. He fisted himself to finish it and endorphins made him dizzy as tension poured out of him, his knees collapsed and he melted down the wall like candle wax into a puddle on the floor.

Stunned, he sat there for a moment dragging in

breaths then looked up at Jules, who wiped her mouth. He'd had many, *many* blow jobs in his life, but never one like that. This woman's mouth should be classified as a lethal weapon, because he felt wrecked inside.

"Were you trying to *kill* me?" he croaked, feeling like she'd stolen his bones.

"Why would I want to do that when it's my turn?" she volleyed, her talented, red-lipstick smeared lips curving into a smile that burned through him. He looked down and saw matching streaks on his cock.

"*Wrong*—it's *my* turn, so you better put on your seat belt," Keegan snarled, pushing up to his feet, his heart still bouncing off his ribs. He was about to give as good as he'd received and then some. Jules Lawson would be calling *him* God by the time he finished.

"Where's the bedroom?" he growled, grabbing her hand.

"The sofa is closer," she replied in a hot whisper, her pupils dilated and her nostrils flared.

***

Jules pried her eyes open and rubbed her face against the hot, smooth skin under her cheek. The delicious masculine morning smell woke her body up better than coffee ever could. She rubbed her leg against the lightly furred calf of a man she was quickly becoming addicted to.

He moaned and his tight muscles quivered under her palm as she skimmed her hand down his body to dive under the sheet. She closed her fingers around his thick erection, ran her thumb over the head and his entire body tensed.

"You're asking for trouble, Natasha," Keegan grumbled in a sleepy sexy morning voice.

She kissed his chest as she stroked him. "If you haven't figured it out by now, Boris, I like trouble. Especially when it comes packaged in a body like yours."

A tremor racked him as he shoved his hand under the sheet to cover hers. He flattened his palm to use her hand to stroke himself twice, then shuddered. "I'd definitely take you up on that, but we have too much to do this morning, baby. I have calls to make."

"Who are you calling?" she mumbled against his skin.

"My buddies. They're trying to get leave so they can go with us," he replied.

"SEAL buddies?" Jules asked, kind of disappointed she'd have to share Keegan with them during the cruise. But she'd have to share him anyway—they were trying to find terrorists and she needed to keep that as her primary focus anyway. A luxury cruise was just their theatre of operations.

"Yeah, you'll like them," he replied as he sighed deeply, before throwing back the covers to sit up. He scrubbed his hands over his face then sucked in a sharp breath. "I forgot about my head. You made me forget last night." He grabbed his phone off her nightstand and scrolled through it. "What the hell do you know? Bledsoe approved all of their chits—after midnight, even.

Probably just to get rid of them." His laugh as he texted his friends danced through her body to settle between her legs where that incredible mouth had been last night.

He dialed a number, then put the phone to his ear as he stood. Jules watched every delicious muscle flex as he bent to snatch up his underwear, before he walked toward the bedroom door.

"Good morning, Commander. I just wanted to make sure you got my message last night, because Ari needs to be taken into federal custody before he has time to talk to his friends. Yeah, the woman and man who were arrested with him, too."

He walked out of the door and Jules stretched her arms over her head then released her breath in a rush. She threw back the covers and got up too, because it looked like she wouldn't be getting a better good morning from her sexy SEAL. There would be plenty of time for that on the cruise, she reminded herself. But now they'd have his buddies with them. Probably in the suite with them.

Mission first, hot sex after, Jules.

If there *was* an after for them, she thought, and the lightness inside of her diminished some as she got out of bed and pulled on her t-shirt and shorts. This could just be a delicious short-term fantasy. Things didn't usually work out long-term for her with men.

This one, who she'd only known a couple of weeks, could show his true colors suddenly and she'd have to sew him into her quilt of could-have-been-great-if-they-hadn't-been-assholes. But damn she definitely

146

didn't want to, because he was so *perfect*. Keegan MacDonald was all the flavors she loved, scooped into the sexiest cone she'd ever had.

Right now she needed to pack, though, and didn't think she had anything remotely resembling cruise clothes in her closet, much less a decent bathing suit. She might have to do some shopping onboard the ship, she thought, walking into her closet to pull out a suitcase.

Since she never spent money on herself and had plenty to spare from her inheritance, she could afford to splurge. No—she deserved to splurge to make this the fantasy of a lifetime. That brought to mind the cost of the cruise. She was going to write Keegan a check for her half of the suite. It was only fair. He'd probably fight her, and if he did, she'd give it to his uncle to make him accept it.

She heard him walk back into the room as he said goodbye to whoever he was talking to. Jules found her suitcase behind her snowshoes and other things at the back of her closet and tugged until it came out. When it did, she fell backwards into a solid brick wall.

"I don't want to be ungentlemanly and steal all the hot water this morning, so you can just shower with me," Keegan said, his hot breath raking the shell of her ear, before he kissed her cheek.

"I have a fifty-gallon tank," Jules replied, and a shiver racked her.

"We'll be able to take a longer shower, then. And we can both fit in this one," he murmured, wrapping his arms around her neck to hug her back into his chest.

Another, more vigorous, tremor shook her when he nipped her earlobe.

"We have to get ready."

"We will be getting ready," he countered, his tongue tracing the rim of her ear. "C'mon, Natasha, live a little. We're going on the vacation of a lifetime, so we need to practice. Everything is set."

This man was so bad—but so incredibly good. How could she resist an offer like that?

Jules added stopping at the drugstore on the way to the port to buy a gross of condoms to her packing list. They would have company in the suite, but they would also have a private bedroom. No dream vacation would be complete without incredible sex with a fantasy man she may have to let go once they got back to port. She had seven amazing days to get her fill of Keegan MacDonald before they got back and she discovered he was a frog.

Why are you so sure he will?

Because nothing in Jules life ever turned out the way she planned. Not her happy life growing up with her parents being there for her, or her fantasy job to avenge their deaths, and certainly not any of the relationships she'd tried to have with men.

Keegan MacDonald was too perfect to be believed, her parents were dead, and her fantasy job turned into a nightmare of sitting in a cubicle, pouring through the financial reports of white-collar criminals, which she would probably be relegated to doing again when she got back home. After not finding the leak at the bar, she knew Brand was in hot water, so there was no way in hell he was going to give her a permanent position. That meant she'd probably be looking for another job too, because ten years of struggling for that position was enough.

Jules hand opened and the suitcase fell on her foot. She turned in Mr. Perfect's arms and his mouth found hers. Live a little is exactly what she was going to do—for ten glorious days with him on a fantasy cruise, which she would remember for the rest of her life. Because, like with her parents, memories might be all she had when she returned.

CHAPTER TWENTY

"Are you sure we're okay getting on board with our weapons?" Jules mumbled to Keegan as she smoothed her loose top over her belly band holster.

"Don't ask, don't tell," he replied, squeezing her shoulders as he smiled down at her. "But if the guys clank when they walk, it's because they had to disassemble their weapons and tape the parts and ammo to their asses. Security has an X-ray for the bags, but not a metal detector."

A laugh burst from her lips and Jules put her arm around his waist to squeeze him back. "I like your friends and I'm glad they're going with us."

"What are we, chopped liver?" Bob asked, glaring down at her. She laughed again when she looked at his wild-flowered shirt. It just didn't fit with his tats and attitude.

"No, you're *family* and I'd have preferred you stay home so you're safe," Keegan replied and Jules' insides melted. "You should've asked before you booked that cabin."

"And you should know better than to try to tell me what to do," Bob growled back. "I only answer to one person and she's standing beside me. Who pulled your frog legs out of the fire last night, boy?"

Keegan sighed. "You did, Uncle Bob—and I thanked you, but it was *stupid* of you and *her* to be there. I'd have figured something out."

"Before or after they dumped your dead body in a ditch somewhere?" Bob asked with a sharp laugh. "If that pretty lady beside *you* hadn't warned me, that's where you'd probably be this morning."

"Can we please just keep our voices down until we're in the suite?" Keegan growled, glancing at the throng of people around them.

"Good to go," Pete Garrison said, as he got back in line and patted his lumpy chest.

"You need a windbreaker, dude," Keegan said, dropping his go bag on the ground to kneel and unzip it. He pulled out a jacket, then handed it to him.

"You don't think wearing a jacket in eighty-degree weather when boarding a cruise ship will be more obvious?" Pete asked with a harsh laugh, as he slid his arms into the sleeves.

Wilson walked up beside Loren. "I told you not to wear that clingy shirt, man. The girls will not be impressed with your man lumps, Baby Gap."

Garrison pinned him with a hot glare. "I don't give a flying fuck about women right now, remember? I had one too many, and now that I'm free? I'm going to have enough beer on this cruise to add a few *natural* lumps to my body so maybe they'll leave me alone for good."

"Bledsoe might have something to say about that," Lawrence said as he joined them in line. He shook his leg and sighed. Keegan looked at him and frowned. "Damn firing pin is poking me in the sack," he explained in a hot whisper out of the corner of his mouth.

"Huddle!" Keegan growled as he hooked his arms

151

through Lawrence and Wilson's arms to drag them away. After an eye roll, Garrison followed them to a far corner of the boarding area, which was the only vacant space in the large room.

"For a man about to embark on a cruise, that boy is wrapped entirely too tight," Louise said after they left. "He needs to learn to relax a little."

"You think he's going to relax on this ship?" Bob asked her, then looked at Jules and a smile eased up the corners of his mouth. "Well, maybe he will a little."

"This is a big deal, Uncle Bob. He's just worried and I am too. Something is—" She looked around her and stopped there. "We need to keep our eyes and ears open and be focused."

Right then, Jules sobered as she remembered why they were standing in line with two thousand other people to board this ship. There were bogies on this passenger list who possibly intended to do people harm, and they were here to find them before that happened.

The four men rejoined them in a much more somber mood and started doing what Jules was doing— looking at every passenger in the holding area to see if she could spot anyone who looked like a potential suspect. Wilson peeled off from the group to do his own thing.

By the time she reached the conveyor belt to put her carry-on bag through X-ray, Jules insides felt like ants were crawling under her skin. Her nerves were at the snapping point as she avoided eye contact with the man standing beside the machine to walk on shaky legs to the other end of the belt and wait for her bag.

Keegan, on the other hand, stopped to shoot the shit with the man, who evidently was ex-Navy, as Wilson, Lawrence, and Garrison put their bags on the belt and quietly came to stand beside her. Once they'd all grabbed their bags, Keegan shook the man's hand and grabbed his own off the belt. Louise and Bob came through behind them and Jules finally breathed again.

"It will be an hour or so before we can go to our suite," Keegan announced, dropping his arm over her shoulders again. "Let's go up on deck and have a drink."

"Sounds like a plan to me," Garrison replied, walking in front of them to the elevator to push the button.

"I definitely need one to calm my nerves about lying to my wife," Lawrence said with a groan. "I'm telling you guys, if you ever tell Lisa I'm on this cruise with you, I will kill you in your sleep. I'm wheels up on a training mission, understand?"

"Misery loves company, so I might tell her. You'll be as divorced as I am, and not so critical of me wanting to drink," Garrison said with a wink.

"Knock it off," Wilson said, his face serious when he returned to the group twenty minutes later. "I've spotted a few possible tangos we need to check out up on deck, so don't be too quick to get mellow."

"Who?" Keegan asked, his smile fading again.

"Sent you photos on your phones. I'm profiling, but I really don't give a damn," he replied. "Download them before we leave port, or will we have WiFi onboard?"

"We'll have a limited package in the suite," Keegan replied.

"We have a *suite*?" Wilson asked with a whistle, his face softening. He looked at Mike and grinned. "Ooh, you're in big trouble if Lisa finds *that* out, Lawrence. She will have your ass drawn and quartered." He puffed out his chest, and smiled. "I'll never have to feel guilty, because I'm staying single forever."

The door opened and Lawrence shoved Wilson inside, then the rest of their group piled in. Jules was sandwiched in the middle, between Keegan and Garrison. Sliding her arms around his waist, she laid her head on his chest and sighed as he rested his hand on her ass. The gesture felt too right to her.

"We'll wait for the next car. There's entirely too much meathead in this elevator," Bob said, stepping back out and giving them the finger as the door slid shut.

God she loved that gruff old man. He was about as real as you could get and what you saw was exactly what you got with him. Just the kind of man Jules had always wanted for herself.

As the doors swept shut, Wilson moved to lean on the wall and Jules heart stopped when the man who'd been with Ari at the bar walked up to stand behind Bob.

CHAPTER TWENTY-ONE

Keegan watched the numbers overhead until they reached the Lido deck and the doors swooshed open. He took Jules' arm and headed for the bar, but she pulled him to the side, in the empty space under the stairway that led up to the sun deck.

"I just saw Abdel," she whispered, and Keegan's insides clenched.

"Where?" he asked, leaning back out to scan the deck.

"Not here—behind Bob when he got back out of the elevator. I saw him just as the doors closed," she said, her voice trembling.

Keegan moved to block her from view. "Did he see you?"

"No, he wasn't looking at me, he was looking at the woman with him. There was another middle-eastern man with him too, or at least I think he was with them," she replied.

Thank goodness they were still docked, Keegan thought, as he pulled out his phone to text Bob. *Follow the Arab men and woman in the elevator with you. Tangos.*

Shit, we just got off on Lido. They went up.

"Stay here," Keegan said, before he walked outside of the stairwell to shade his eyes and look up to see what was above the main deck. His eyes snagged on a sun deck just outside of the bridge which was probably for VIP guests. That would be the perfect place to have both a bird's-eye view of the Lido deck and the crew on the bridge.

He would bet that was where they were headed.

Since he had booked the best suite on the ship, he would also bet they could get passes up to that sundeck, too. The problem was he knew he and Jules would be recognized. Bob and Louise had a suite as well, so they could probably go up there and observe.

He moved back into the shade to text Bob.

Go to the guest services desk and get passes to the VIP deck outside of the bridge. I think that's where they're going. Listen in and get a photo of them if you can.

Roger that—but we are getting a drink first!

He pocketed his phone then walked back under the stairwell. "Put your sunglasses back on," he said, pulling his own out of his pocket to put them on. She unzipped her bag, dug inside, and then slid them on.

"Where are we going?" she asked as he grabbed her hand and dragged her back on deck.

"We're going to sit out here and see who shows up on that sun deck up by the bridge. After the muster drill, we're going see if the shops are open, because we both need disguises now."

And like it or not, you need to stay in the room more often than not. He would make sure that someone was in there with her at all times. This is the man who'd tried to kill her at the bar, and Keegan didn't doubt he'd try again if he saw her. It would be very easy to do once they were at sea, so from here on out, she would not be out of his sight.

As soon as they finished the safety drill, Keegan led Jules to the bar and asked the bartender on which deck he could find the shops. Instead of taking the elevator where they might be seen, because passengers were now going to their rooms, he zigzagged through hallways until he found the stairwell at the back of the ship.

"After that trek, we have to go down four flights of stairs?" she asked when he took the first step. "Why can't we just take the elevator?"

"You want to be trapped in an elevator with Abdel?" he asked, shaking his head.

"No, I guess you're right," she replied, her lips pinched as she followed behind him as he practically ran down the stairs. When they reached the landing on the fourth flight, she stopped to catch her breath. "Remind me to wear tennis shoes tomorrow, okay?"

"You need to do more cardio, Natasha," he said with a grin. "Naked and in heels. And I get to watch." He waggled his eyebrows and she slugged him in the arm.

"Only if you do it first," she said, sliding off her heels to dangle them from her fingers. "These things are torture devices invented by men because they don't have to wear them."

"You're probably right," he agreed, his grin inching up. "Because we like to watch the amazing things they do for your ass."

"My ass looks amazing even without them, thank you." She breezed past him, putting some extra action in the backfield. His eyes locked on the hem of her short, swingy, floral-print dress and his tongue flapped out.

"Yes, it does," he mumbled as he followed her.

At the end of the hall, they took a left down the wide corridor and walked along a row of very expensive looking shops. They passed a salon and she stopped to peer inside.

"I could always get my hair cut and colored," she suggested, looking up at him. "Wearing those extensions your aunt gave me last night kind of gave me the fever to do something different."

"*No*—we'll just get a hat and scarf," he growled, reaching out to run the long silky blonde strands through his fingers. That hot silk felt incredible against his skin when she had him in her sassy, wet mouth last night. He went rock-hard as he dropped her hair and stepped back.

Jesus, was sex with her all he could think about now?

"Let's see if they have something temporary," she said, lifting a brow as she walked inside, even after what he'd said.

Two hours later, he walked out of the salon with a redhead and enough pent-up drive to nail her into the wooden floor beneath his feet. Keegan only thought she was sexy as a blonde. If she wanted to *not* attract attention, auburn was not the color choice he'd have suggested. Her blue eyes jumped out of her face now and the ends of the chin length bob pointed directly to her mouth, which made him want to slam her against the wall and kiss her.

Instead, he followed her to the last clothing store on the row, which, from the sari-wrapped mannequin in the window, appeared to offer standard cruise fare inside. His mind conjured images of him removing that vibrant yellow, orange and green dress with the exotic parrot print that only wrapped around her delicious body and knotted at her shoulder.

It would be like opening the best birthday present he'd ever gotten. Before they left the store he was going to buy her that dress, he thought walking inside behind her.

Maybe not—they were trying to blend in, he reminded himself, as he strode to the back where the hats were located. Jules went to the other side of the store, leaving him to choose a hat for her. He grabbed a couple of ball caps for himself then turned around to look at the ladies' section and chose a huge, floppy straw-colored hat with a bright pink ribbon.

When he turned around to show it to her, his eyes ping-ponged around, but he couldn't find her. He dropped the hats and frantically searched around the circular racks but she was not inside the store. His insides clenched and his blood turned to ice in his veins as he strode out in the corridor to look up and down for her.

A rush of fear paralyzed him as he couldn't decide whether to go left or right. A waterfall of relief, which quickly turned to anger, rushed through him when a flash of red caught his attention in the swimsuit shop across the hall. The floor rumbled, then moved under his feet as he walked toward the shop.

They were underway, trapped for ten days with a terrorist on board. His stomach knotted as he second guessed his decision to come on this trip. He had a very bad feeling since they boarded—one he hadn't had since he left the teams. They were about to be caught up in a goat fuck of epic proportions, but it was too late to do anything about it.

CHAPTER TWENTY-TWO

"Can't I go out on deck?" Jules asked for the hundredth time, this time from the sliding glass door that led out to their private balcony. "The hot tub is nice, but it's hot out here and I'd really like to get into the pool. We didn't even get off the ship in Bermuda. Are we getting off in Tortola like we planned?"

"No, we're not. Everything we need is right in here. I'll take you surfing in Virginia Beach when we get home," Keegan replied, frantically texting Greg Lambert the photos the guys had gathered. "This suite is intended for us not to have to leave until we dock. If you need something, just call room service."

"We could've stayed holed up in my room at home, MacDonald. We're here to find a terrorist and we're not doing that by staying cooped up in here."

Do not look at her Keegan—she's changed into that swimsuit again.

"Bob and Louise have been watching Abdel up on the sun deck and the guys are following him and his cohorts wherever they go." But that was useless, since none of them spoke Arabic, which the men had kept to in all conversations.

Keegan had asked the Commander if he could have a linguist join them at one of the ports, but, so far, he hadn't found one. Greg Lambert was fully on board with giving them what they needed after he verified the man in the photo Bob snapped was Abdel Nour.

Since they were in international waters and would be until they returned to Baltimore, however, he couldn't be arrested. They were just supposed to watch him closely and take him into custody when they got back to Baltimore. Lambert said he still wasn't sold on the terrorist threat, and honestly, neither was Keegan yet.

Would Abdel be on a boat he planned on hijacking or destroying?

No, he would not. Nour was the mastermind of all the evil carried out by his organization. He had underlings and jihadists to do the dirty work for him, which could possibly be the roles of the other men on board with him. Keegan wouldn't know that for sure until Greg provided ID from the photos.

"Well, if you decide you want to rub oil on my back for me, I'll just be out here," she said in a petulant tone as he heard the door roll open, but he didn't dare look. Jules Lawson was determined to torture and distract him and it was working.

They would be in Tortola in the morning, and he *really* wanted to take her surfing as he promised, but he wasn't sure they should disembark there, either. Taking the chance that Abdel would recognize her just wasn't worth it.

You paid ten thousand dollars for a fucking vacation and you need to have one.

Yes, he did, he thought, throwing his phone on the coffee table with a disgusted grunt. If four Navy SEALs and a retired Ranger couldn't protect her, who could? In fact, he was going to get Jules right now and they *were* going up on deck. Keegan stood, but groaned when his phone dinged. He picked it up again and quickly opened the text.

Abbad Salam, Al Qaeda lieutenant, female is Irshal, his wife. Second and third man unknown. Linguist will join you on Tortola. Arranged cover for her with cruise line admin and she will contact you once onboard.

Thank God for that, but the confirmation those men were radicals only made the band of tension around his chest tighter. Adding that to what Jules overheard, and that those men were gathered on this ship, it was obvious they weren't here for a vacation. But until the interpreter joined them, they wouldn't know what they were plotting.

All he could do was watch and wait now. And stop hiding in his freaking cabin when he was on a luxury vacation with a beautiful woman.

Keegan walked to the slider, opened it with purpose and spotted Jules sunning herself and reading on a chaise at the end of the long balcony. He strode to the chair, and snatched the magazine from her hand. She pushed her floppy hat back and he could feel her glare at him through her sunglasses.

"What? Are you taking my magazine too, Boris? Am I in time out or something?"

He grabbed her hand and pulled her to her feet. "No, Natasha, you are going up on that deck with me and we are going swimming, if that bikini doesn't start a riot."

She harrumphed, and traced the indention at the bottom of his throat with a finger. "I didn't even think you noticed."

"Baby, I noticed. Every. Damned. Thing. About. You. Even when I don't want to."

He snatched the hat from her head, gripped the back of her head with his other hand and pulled her mouth to his. She sighed into his mouth, wound her arms around his neck and her nipples hardened against his chest.

Keegan dropped her hat to grip her ass and pull her flush to his painful erection. When she ground her hips against him and mewled into his mouth, he knew they wouldn't be making it to the pool deck any time soon.

He dragged his mouth from hers, then bent and swept her up in his arms. After two steps toward nirvana, he stopped when his phone dinged again like a freaking cash register.

"Not looking," he said when he met her frustrated eyes. Her wide smile lit up his insides as he carried her inside and walked directly toward their posh bedroom.

The front door of the suite beeped, which meant someone was crashing their party. Why in the hell had he invited them to come with him? *Because you need their help.* With a sigh, Keegan eased Jules to her feet and turned as Lawrence rushed inside.

"Bob saw a money transfer. Isn't that part of what Jules overheard?" he asked, striding over to them.

"Yes, it is," Jules replied in a tight voice.

"How does he know it was a money transfer?" Keegan asked.

"Abdel met some guy, a Latin man he hadn't met with before, up on the sun deck. He dropped a pretty large duffle on the ground beside his chair. They had drinks and he left without it. The other guy picked it up and walked away with it."

"Did Bob get a photo of the Latin guy?" Keegan asked.

"Said he couldn't because they would've noticed. They sat too close to him and Louise. But they spoke in English, so he heard what they said. Something is being loaded on the ship at one of our stops before getting back to Baltimore."

"That's what I heard Ari and Abdel talking about at the bar," Jules confirmed in a shaky voice. "What I suspected has to be true, then. I wonder which port?"

Tortola. Dominican Republic. Which would it be? Or had it already been loaded on the ship in Bermuda? *Fuck, they should've gotten off the ship in Bermuda.*

But surely Abdel's partner would've wanted the money up front—before the goods or services were rendered—whatever they were. These were criminals, terrorists, and thugs they were talking about, so trust wasn't part of the equation. That meant most likely the *package* hadn't been loaded on the ship yet.

Keegan's body wilted with relief. But Jules was right—hiding in this room was not finding them, or identifying the threat. There wouldn't be surfing, scuba diving, or beachcombing on this trip, but Keegan would make it up to Jules later.

165

From here on out, it would be all hands and eyes on deck when they docked, to observe the loading process. Keegan wished like hell he could fill in the Captain and crew about the potential threat, but he couldn't risk it.

"Can't we alert the Captain and crew about the situation now?" Jules asked, as if reading his mind.

"No, we don't have enough evidence," Keegan replied, with a sigh. "And if something is being loaded on this ship, we don't know that one of the crew isn't involved in the plan." Keegan looked at his friend. "Lawrence, round up the others and come back so we can have a SITREP and make assignments for the rest of the cruise."

The only question in his mind at the moment was how many people were at risk here—two thousand on the passenger list, or two million on the east coast? To impress the whole east coast, as Jules heard Ari and Abdel discuss at the bar, it would have to be one hell of a *party*, so he would bet on the latter.

That meant they were probably talking about a bomb.

CHAPTER TWENTY-THREE

"Nothing out of the ordinary and forward bay is buttoned up," Wilson murmured as he walked up beside Keegan at the second loading area aft on the ship. "Lawrence and Gars are down checking the hull. Bob saw Godzilla leave the ship when we docked this morning, so he's following him."

Day before yesterday, it had almost killed him having to stand on the dock in Tortola and watch the waves crashing into the nearby shore. But he'd done it, and so had Jules to give him cover as they strolled back and forth along the pier. Nothing had been loaded on that ship that day, he knew that for sure.

Today, she and Louise decided to stay in the cabin, and he didn't blame them.

It had to happen here—the Dominican Republic was their last stop. Unless they'd missed it in Bermuda and the device was already onboard. Keegan just couldn't get that out of his mind. One of the jihadists could have managed to smuggle something on the ship. That was a possibility, too. They'd smuggled small automatic rifles, hadn't they? A dirty bomb could fit in a suitcase—but probably not one that would do the damage they were talking about—and it would've had to go through the X-ray.

Keegan looked back at the fork trucks, which were steadily moving crates of food and supplies onto the ship. Any one of those crates could hold enough explosives to take out this vessel, and more. It was like finding a needle in a hundred-ton haystack.

"We've got to try to search the ship. We know what cabins the tangos are in, so we should start there. Maybe find some crew uniforms, so we can move around easier," Keegan said.

"I'll catch up with the guys and see what we can do," Lawrence said as he strode toward the gangway.

Other than entertaining Wilson, the navy officer Greg sent as an interpreter, who met them in Tortola, had been a waste. In her defense, the deal was done by the time she got on the ship and they hadn't seen the suspects meet again.

She found out what kind of wine Abdel liked with dinner by serving them in the main dining room, but other than that, nothing. He looked down the dock and saw Wilson and Gars walking toward them, drying off with towels and carrying their snorkeling gear. Gars gave him the all clear sign before they walked up the gangplank to re-board.

Keegan looked at his watch and saw it was almost time for the ship to leave. Bob wasn't back yet, which worried him. He took out his phone to text him, but remembered Bob's phone was off because they didn't have service in port. It was stupid to let his uncle go off alone, following one of the most dangerous men on the planet, but there just wasn't anyone to spare to go with him. Louise offered to go, but he refused and he was stubborn enough to win that argument. Her last words, said in anger to him, "*Well go ahead and get your stupid ass killed. Your life insurance is paid up,*" rang inside of Keegan's skull.

If those words came to pass, he knew it would crush his aunt. He had never known a married couple who loved each other more than them, even his own parents. Bob and Louise MacDonald argued hard, but they loved harder and were perfect for one another.

A lot like you and Jules Lawson.

No time to be going there now, MacDonald.

After the last crate was loaded into the hatch, the dock workers closed it and moved their equipment. Keegan looked at the re-boarding line, which was getting longer by the second and headed that way to see if his uncle was there. When he got to the last person in line, his worry notched up to the yellow zone. When he saw the dock attendant close the gate, it went into full red alert. Keegan took off running toward the gate, but stopped when a taxi came to a screeching, sliding stop at the curb and Bob flew out of the back door.

When he got closer, Keegan saw his bloody face, his bloodier knuckles and the fear on his face. "Let me in, moron!" he shouted at the guard, grabbing the gate to rattle it.

The guard took a step back and folded his arms. "With that attitude, I think you need to be a *guest* here for a few days to learn some manners. It looks like some of the locals have started those lessons, eh?" Keegan hurried to the gate to intervene.

"My uncle is obviously distressed and in need of medical attention," Keegan said, moving to stand in front

169

of the guard. "I'm sure he'll apologize, if you give him a second to catch his breath." He turned to glare at Bob. "Isn't that right, Uncle Bob?"

Bob huffed a deep breath. "Yes, I'm *sorry*. Will you *please* let me in so I don't miss my ship, mo—ah, *sir?*" he growled, but the guard didn't budge, he just stared at Bob.

"Try again, Unk!" Keegan shouted, grinding his teeth.

"Look—I've had a *really* bad day in your beautiful country. If you let me through that gate, I promise I will *never* be back here to bother you again."

Keegan knew that was as good as he was going to give, so he worked on Plan B in his mind as the guard just continued to stare at his uncle. The ship's horn blew, and Keegan knew his time was up. He didn't want to—but he had no choice. He turned back toward the ship, moved past the guard then turned and put a blood choke on the guard. The man clawed at his arm, tried to twist out of Keegan's hold, but he held tight until the man passed out.

When he released him, his shoulder told him that was a terrible idea. It felt like the joint was out of place and shards of searing pain streaked down his arm, until they hit the numb spot on the side of his hand.

"Well, fuck me," he growled, holding his arm as he fished the key out of the guard's pocket with his left hand. His hand shook as he opened the gate, tossed the keys down beside the prone man then took off running for the gangway, which they were preparing to lift. He heard Bob running behind him and sent up thanks.

"Two more—*wait!*" he shouted, and breathed when the dock worker stopped unwinding the anchor rope from the piling.

Keegan's shoulder was on fire as he ran up the gangway and handed his on board account card to the crew member who checked him back in. Bob did the same and they went through security. When they got to the elevator and the hatch closed, he turned to glare at Bob.

"What in the ever loving hell have you been doing?!?" he grated.

"Making sure Godzilla didn't get away," Bob replied, with a grin. His split lip opened and blood coated his teeth. "There were a few hitches in that plan, but I survived."

"What did you do?" Keegan asked with a groan.

"I escorted him to the U.S. Embassy," Bob replied proudly. "His associate wasn't too keen on the idea, but he finally saw things my way."

His uncle was fucking *brilliant*—that's all there was to it.

A rush of emotion surged through him as he hugged Bob with his good arm. "Have I told you how much I love you lately, Unk?"

"No, but you better love me plenty. I think I broke my fucking hand on that guy's face," he said, rubbing his rapidly swelling right hand.

"You didn't tuck your thumb, did you? Keegan

asked with a laugh, as they walked into the elevator. "Hell, you taught me not to do that when I was ten."

"Yep, sure did. It's been too damned long since I was in a good fight so I forgot. But it was worth it. That big bastard fell hard and the other smaller one is where he belongs."

Keegan just hoped the rest of this operation ended so well, because they had a lot of area to cover, only seven people to do the searching and two days at sea before they reached Baltimore.

CHAPTER TWENTY-FOUR

"We're twelve hours out of Baltimore and we're only halfway done with our search. I'm bored and could help if you let me," Jules said, blowing out a breath.

With every second that ticked off the clock, every nautical mile they got closer to Baltimore, the tension inside him grew. Keegan still didn't know if they were going to blow up the ship to kill the two thousand passengers on board, or if they planned to wait until they were in the harbor for something much grander.

Evidence or not, it was probably time to alert the Captain. From a public relations standpoint, the cruise line may or may not do anything about it anyway, without evidence. Freaking out two thousand wealthy guests on a boutique cruise line could be very bad for business, if it turned out to be nothing.

In five hours, they'd be in US waters so he could tell Commander Lambert to alert the Navy and Coast Guard, if *they* would do anything without evidence. Hell, the photos he sent to Greg should be enough. The fact that five known terrorists had been on this ship and three left the ship before it returned to port should be enough.

Keegan was very afraid it wouldn't be enough.

Playing devil's advocate to see it from Greg and the military's perspective, the tangos could've been on vacation and Keegan could be just looking for terror plots where none existed to find excitement, since he was now a washed up SEAL.

"Maybe I was wrong and this *is* about caviar and champagne for a party," Jules said, her voice trembling. "I could be wrong, you know."

"No, they wouldn't want to kill us if that were the case," Keegan replied, pulling off his hat to run a hand through his hair. "It's the only explanation."

She walked her fingers up his arm to the padded shoulder of his white coat and squeezed the cap. He flinched as shards of white hot pain sliced down his arm.

"How's your shoulder? Why don't you take off your coat and shirt so I can put another ice pack on it?"

Garrison helped him put his shoulder back in place last night and Jules applied ice packs all night, even while he was sleeping. It felt marginally better this morning as long as he kept his arm at his side. He just hoped he didn't have reason to fire his pistol today, because he wasn't sure he could grip it.

"It's fine—I don't have time. I just got frustrated and had to come back here to think for a minute." Jules wasn't making that easy by twisting her fingers in the hair at his nape.

"What are you thinking about?" Jules asked, and agitation rippled through him. "Why aren't you including me in things and what aren't you telling me?"

I'm thinking that I need to focus and you are hell bent on distracting me. The last time he let a woman do that during a mission is why his shoulder was fucked up and he was off the teams. Keegan needed to remember that.

"Now that Abdel is off the ship, you can help us search." *So maybe you'll give me five feet of breathing room to reason this out and plan.* "I found out that Abbad Salam and

174

his wife didn't re-board the ship either, so that leaves us with only two men to surveil, but so far we can't find either of them, or the bomb. They didn't leave the ship, but disappeared."

"Have I told you how hot you look in that uniform? I bet you looked hotter in your dress whites with all those medals I'm sure you earned." She cradled his jaw in her hands and rubbed her thumb over his beard stubble. When he went rock-hard, his insides twisted. "You'll have to pull them out and model them for me one day."

He turned his face away. "I need to think, Jules."

She pulled her hand off his shoulder and sat up. "Do you *think* maybe they had the same idea we did? That they stole uniforms to blend in so they're ready to do whatever they have planned?"

That could definitely explain their disappearance. With a crew of one thousand from all nationalities, who all resembled each other in uniform, they could blend in as easily as their team had. If he was a terrorist looking to hide out, that's exactly what he would have done.

"Other than the remainder of the staterooms, where else do we need to search?" Jules asked.

"The kitchen and the bridge," he replied, trying but failing to keep the sharpness from his tone. "The kitchen staff wear different uniforms than the rest of the crew, though, so I'll have to *requisition* those. It will be tough going to search there and not to be noticed, because it's staffed twenty-four hours." *And I need you to back off, so I can work out how we're going to search there without spending the rest of the cruise in the brig for trespassing.*

Maybe it was time for him to at least talk to the Captain. But what would he say? I think your ship might be under terrorist attack so you should take action to protect the passengers? Evidence? Oh, no, sir, I don't have any evidence, but you should just trust my gut feeling.

Yeah, he knew how that scenario would work out.

"Let's go out on deck," he said, standing and holding his hand out to Jules. She uncurled her legs and took his hand to stand.

"After this is over, I'm paying for us to go back to Tortola to surf, Boris. I hear there are naked beaches there. You ever surfed naked?" she said, walking with him toward the slider.

"Can't say that I have," he replied, opening the glass door as snapshots of her on a board without a stitch, her wet skin glistening in the tropical sun, almost brought him to his knees.

Fuck—stop it, MacDonald. He walked to the rail, sucked it a deep breath to cool his insides and his libido. This was not the time, but he had no control over it. His fantasy slipped the leash and he chased it into the surf.

Everything about this woman excited and distracted him, and that was fine, as long as he wasn't worried about saving thousands of lives. The way Jules Lawson thought was different from any other woman he'd ever known. She was not only beautiful and smart, she knew how to live. Surfing, riding a bike, diving head-first into danger to avenge her parents' deaths? All of his own favorite flavors wrapped up into the most delicious woman he'd ever had.

Most women didn't seek out adventure and danger, but Jules seemed to thrive on it. Her parents and brother's lives being cut so short affected her deeply, and was probably a major factor in her wanting to squeeze every ounce out of life. But the thought of her continuing to take those adventures alone made his insides twist.

Keegan hoped after this was over, she'd seek out a nice desk job somewhere safe. They had no ties yet really, but he couldn't help but hope he would be around to protect her from herself. He wanted to be on that quest for adventure with her. To crawl inside her delicious body and live there to soak up everything she had to offer.

But first, he had to get them out of this situation alive. And then he had to find the balls to tell her that he thought he was falling in love with her. That would be the sticker because the last woman he'd said that to had kicked him in the teeth.

Never in his wildest imagination did he think he'd be saying those words to a woman again. Especially not so soon. Being *with* a woman like her would definitely make being *off* the teams more bearable.

"It's so beautiful out here," Jules said with a soulful sigh as she walked up beside him. "I wish we had more time to enjoy it."

177

"Me, too, baby," Keegan said sliding his left arm around her. "I promise we'll do something to make up for this—" Keegan's stomach clenched, pinching off his words as the ship rocked and he realized it had just slowed down to a crawl.

His leaned over the railing and looked toward the bow, where he saw a pilot boat headed toward them. Their guide through the Chesapeake channel into to the harbor was probably on board. The smaller boat bobbed violently in the ship's wake then swung wide to match up and pull aside. The single door on the pilot boat cabin opened and a man in black BDUs walked across the deck to the ladder holding something to his side. He grabbed the rung near his head and climbed up to the deck.

Keegan expected the pilot boat to pull off, but it stayed. Another man dressed the same as the first appeared on deck and rushed to climb the ladder too. When two more followed, Keegan knew the party had just started and it was time to get dressed to meet the new arrivals.

CHAPTER TWENTY-FIVE

Keegan's insides buzzed as he hung up the phone after leaving a message for Greg Lambert to get the Coast Guard and Navy on standby in Baltimore. He gave the Commander a SITREP and told him they needed backup, but not until after they neutralized the threat in the wheelhouse. Then they could safely offload the passengers into lifeboats as calmly as possible.

He hoped like hell Greg Lambert wasn't in one of those infamous and useless all-day-long meetings at the Pentagon, which was usually followed by a half-the-night drinks and dinner recap. That was the only reason he could think of as to why the man's phone would be off.

Since the tangos had most likely taken over the bridge by now, which Wilson and Garrison were verifying, talking to the Captain to get the crew's assistance wasn't an option. If the Coast Guard and Navy charged in before they regained control of the bridge and neutralized the threat, it would only get people killed.

Keegan wondered why the group had brought more men onto the ship if they just planned on detonating a bomb in Baltimore Harbor. Why they would need those men to navigate to Inner Harbor where the ship's bridge crew were already headed, via the Chesapeake channel?

Maybe they planned on running this ship into the cruise terminal. Although, impressive, that wasn't a 9/11 scale statement.

Think bigger, Keegan. A big gesture that would impress everyone on the east coast and would need more men to make sure it happened. Holy shit!

The White House was only twenty miles overland from Chesapeake Bay, near Edgewater. The bridge crew would not stop the ship until they reached Inner Harbor—but if the jihadists stopped it there and detonated a sizable bomb, it could do some serious damage to Capitol Hill.

If they ran the ship up the Potomac Channel to the Naval Shipyard, which was a little dicier, they could even get closer to the White House and probably take out most of The Hill with the bomb.

Keegan would just about bet that was their plan. Al Qaeda's one failure during the 9/11 attacks was the plane that went down in Pennsylvania, instead of reaching its target, which everyone suspected was the White House.

Keegan's blood ran cold and his stomach lurched.

Please, Lord don't let it be a dirty bomb. Just regular C-4 and we can deal with this.

Or he thought they could. If they could find it and disarm it in time.

The door to the suite slammed back on its hinges and Wilson walked in looking dire. "Shit just got real, MacDaddy. They executed the Captain right in front of the others on the bridge and the ship is moving again. We'll be in the Chesapeake channel in two hours.

"Lawrence is searching the port kitchen. I need you to go starboard and see if you can find anything. Is Gars still on point at the bridge?"

"Yeah, he's doing recon from the sun deck, but can't bring his weapon out or it will freak out the passengers. It's in his go bag with mine."

"I'll assemble mine and find Gars. You find that bomb, *now*."

"Aye, Boss," Wilson said with a wink as he spun on his heel to leave the suite.

"What can I do to help, Son?" Bob asked, walking up to him. "I'm old but, as you know now, I'm not out."

"You and Louise know the faces of the two men who were already on board best. Try to find them, if you can. Since we've scoured the upper decks, I'd try the lower decks."

"Aye, Boss," Bob mimicked Wilson, then held out his arm to his wife. "Let's go, Louise—we have some terrorists to find."

"You won't hear me say this often, old man, but I'm scared out of my tree right now," Louise said as she took his arm.

"I'll protect you, babe," he said, dropping a kiss on her forehead. "You just stand back and watch me in action."

They left the suite, then Jules stepped up to him. "I'm scared, too. What can I do to help? Do you really think they plan on detonating the bomb in the harbor?" she asked.

Keegan looked into her eyes, swam in their beautiful blue depths for a minute, then decided he couldn't let the last thing he might say to her be a lie. Fear or not, she deserved to know what he really thought.

"No, I don't think that's the plan."

"What is it, then?" she asked, her eyes widening.

"You said they were going for a grand gesture. Blowing up the White House and Capitol Hill is about as grand as they can get. It's only twenty miles overland from the Chesapeake, or if they want to go for maximum damage, five miles taking the Potomac to the Navy Shipyard."

"Oh, my God," she said, her face blanching as she put a trembling hand over her mouth.

"Yeah, we've got to stop them." Keegan pulled out his phone and called Greg Lambert to update him on what he thought was going down.

The Secret Service needed to secure the President and personnel at the White House immediately in case they couldn't stop them in time. He also added a second request to hold back the cavalry until they could get the situation under control, but he doubted that was an option now without an order from on high.

If Greg got his message in time. If he didn't, they would be coming into the channel at night and nobody would see them until the fireworks went off.

CHAPTER TWENTY-SIX

Keegan's fingers gripped the armrests of his chair so hard, it felt like they might crumble in his hands. Well, his left hand, anyway. All he was accomplishing with his right was enflaming the nerve in his arm up to his shoulder. He released his grip and flexed his fingers in his lap to try to get the feeling back.

Now that night had fallen, the crowd on the deck was elbow-to-elbow, dancing and partying. The blaring reggae music would help them cover the sound of gunfire, but the size of the crowd could mean more casualties. To minimize that possibility, they had to be surgically precise when they stormed that bridge and attract as little attention as possible.

"When are we going to call the guys back so we can handle this situation?" Wilson asked tersely. "Are we just going to wait for them to kill someone else?"

"We can't go in yet, because we don't want to lose the element of surprise, but we have to act soon," Garrison replied. "We need to get Lawrence up here, and flesh this out."

"I sent Jules to go find him a few minutes ago. They should be back soon," Keegan replied, itching to reach inside his go bag to pull out his rifle and kill every one of those radical bastards.

This—*this* is why he joined the teams—to take out these threats to his country. Right now, though, he felt powerless to do anything but watch the jihadists systematically slaughter the people on the bridge.

So far, they'd murdered three of the crew,

including the Captain. It had been two hours since he left those messages for Greg Lambert and their time was running out. They were at the mouth of the Chesapeake now, and once they entered the channel, launching lifeboats to offload passengers would be more difficult.

Bob suddenly appeared beside him looking extremely angry. "I found one of the rat bastards near the hold and he's tied up in the suite," he informed gruffly. "I also located the interpreter and she's grilling him, but I'm going back to give him a little more incentive to talk." He handed Keegan a pair of ship radios. "Louise and I *requisitioned* these from the crew storage locker. Thought they might help you keep an eye on the bridge. Channel 21 is clear, 16 is for crew com. Louise and I have one too, so hit me up, if you need me."

"Sir, you can serve on my team any time," Gars said, grinning from ear-to-ear as he reached out to snatch one of the radios and shove an ear plug into his ear. "*You* are the MacDaddy, and Keegan is a trainee."

With a snort and an eye roll, Bob handed the second radio to Keegan and hurried back toward the elevators.

That's exactly how Keegan felt at the moment. Like a tadpole back in BUDs training, trying to pass the drown-proofing test. Definitely in over his head. But he would fake it until he made it, keep pushing up from the bottom, because failure in this test had the same consequences.

"I didn't find anything so far. Wilson said he

184

didn't either. Are we going in now?" Lawrence asked, walking up to them with Jules tagging behind. He dropped his go bag on the floor beside a chair and it clanked. Wilson took a seat beside Garrison, and hefted his bag up onto his lap.

"Yeah, we can't wait anymore," Keegan replied, standing. "We need to try to take at least one of them alive so we can find out where that bomb is located."

"Since the tangos are wearing black and the crew white, we shouldn't have a problem getting a fix on them once we enter. We need to go in low so they don't get a fix on us and so we don't shoot each other," Lawrence said, standing again.

Garrison stood too, and picked up his bag. "There are two entry points, one on either side of the bridge," he said.

"Lawrence and I will take the starboard side, you and Wilson take port. Let's turn the radios on 21. I'll give you a go signal when we're ready," Keegan said, bending to grab his bag. When his shoulder gave out, he dropped it and rubbed until the ache subsided.

"Dude, I think you should sit this one out. Go back to the suite with Bob and get what you can from the tango," Wilson said, his eyes focused on Keegan's hand. "There are only four of them—we've got this."

Because if he went in there and his arm malfunctioned, he could endanger them all. He was a liability to them now, which is why he was no longer needed on the teams. Those black clouds gathered in his head again and his ego sank to fill the toes of his boots. Having Jules here to witness it made his humiliation complete.

Not now, MacDonald—do what's best for your team. You can fall apart later. This isn't about you, or your ego, it's about a successful operation with no casualties and you can't guarantee that if you go with them. His teeth hurt as he ground them before he nodded and held out his fist.

"Hooyah," he said, his eyes burning fiercely. The other men looked relieved as they all bumped fists with him.

"As soon as we have control, we'll sound the abandon ship alert," Garrison said after bumping knuckles with him. "You be a hero and help Bob find out where that bomb is so we can disarm it." Because he might not be fifty-eight years old, but he was just as useless to them.

He couldn't stay to watch the action, so with his chest tighter than it had ever been, he turned and strode to the elevators. After he pushed the button, his phone vibrated in his pocket and he pulled it out.

Maverick and Wingman are secure. Cavalry is on go at your command—setting up eight miles out. Covert team with Fido on the way to board for assist. Don't fuck this up or God will rain fire down on my head.

If Keegan fucked this up, fire would be raining down on *everyone's* head.

He was just relieved that the President and Vice

President were safe. News that they would soon have more help—and a bomb sniffing dog—was welcome.

Roger that and thanks. Hooyah.

CHAPTER TWENTY-SEVEN

Jules felt as useless as a Band-Aid on a bullet hole as she watched Keegan and Bob, through the interpreter, grill the man they had duct taped to a chair. Even with threats of killing him, though, they had gotten nothing out of him yet.

She had a few ideas to speed the process along, because she'd studied these assholes after they killed her parents, to find out exactly how they ticked. But she wasn't willing to be told she was a distraction again. So here she sat on the sofa, twiddling her thumbs.

Twenty minutes later, when she couldn't take it anymore, she stood and walked to Keegan's duffle bag and rifled through it. Badass Navy SEALs always had a knife, right? She found his at the bottom of the bag and carefully released the long, pointy and razor sharp blade then walked over to them.

"Don't you get that he *wants* to die?" she asked brusquely. "If he dies, he's a martyr and gets seventy-two virgins when he meets the devil he worships. He knows the bomb will kill him anyway and is okay with that, or he wouldn't be on this ship." She nudged Keegan aside and looked at the interpreter. "After I stick this knife into the chair between his balls, tell him I'm going to pin them to the chair with it next, if he doesn't tell us where that bomb is located. Tell him he won't have anything left to fuck his seventy-two virgins with by the time I'm done with him."

His eyes widened, focused on the knife and he whimpered when she arced the knife and planted it in the chair so close to his balls she probably sliced the seam of his pants. Jules stood and glared at him as the interpreter spoke.

Beads of sweat formed at his hairline and he swallowed hard as he met her eyes. "Yes, I'm serious, asshole. I'm going to cut your fucking head off after you bleed to death and throw it overboard too, so there will be no paradise for you."

"Damn, you're brutal, and I have to say that's sexy as hell, Natasha," Keegan mumbled behind her.

"Don't try and suck up now, Boris. You and I need to have a talk when this is over," she fired back. "I do have a brain. I don't need you to protect me. And sometimes a female perspective is a valuable asset when you're not a sexist pig."

He'd excluded her from every aspect of this operation so far, and Jules was tired of it. He called her a partner, but he'd mostly kept her locked up in this room. If he didn't trust her enough to be his partner because he thought he was so badass he didn't need her, then she didn't need him. Maybe he wasn't as perfect as she thought he was. Maybe he was just another mistake in a long line of mistakes she thought she'd put behind her.

When the interpreter stopped talking, the terrorist looked at Jules again, then turned to the interpreter and started talking.

"*Yesss!*" Keegan hissed, grabbing her shoulders but she pulled away.

The interpreter turned to face them with stark

terror in her dark eyes. "He says the bombs are in the engine room, the hold, and the kitchen area."

"*Bombs?!?*" Keegan, Bob and Jules shouted in unison.

"Are they C-4 or nuclear?" Keegan asked, walking over to pull the knife out of the chair. "*Ask* him!" he shouted, when she froze.

He met the man's eyes, raised the knife and the interpreter mouthed the words in a trembling voice. When he didn't answer immediately, Keegan brought the knife down. At the very last second, he squealed out, "*Chemical!* C-4 and sarin gas."

"Find out when and how they will detonate," Keegan instructed, standing again.

The interpreter asked the jihadi and he glanced at Keegan's hand before answering.

"What did he say?" he asked.

"He says his partner will detonate the bombs when the ship stops," the interpreter replied, her voice choked. "Can we get off the ship? Use the life boats? I have a daughter."

"Not if we can't stop. Ask him what his target was," Keegan demanded, and Jules held her breath.

He glanced at Keegan, then said, "The White House." Keegan turned and looked green as his hand opened and the knife fell to the carpet.

The ship's radio that Keegan left on the coffee table keyed. "Bridge is secure. Four tangos down—one unaccounted. No casualties. We are halfway down the channel and need to offload these passengers so we can turn around pronto. Brothers just boarded."

He walked over to grab the radio.

"We can't stop, Gars, or the unaccounted will detonate. Chemical, C-4, and Sarin. Three devices. One in the hold, one in the kitchen, and one in the engine bay. Get whoever knows how to use those Azipod-thrusters to turn us back to sea. Alert the crew to man the muster stations and be prepared to start evac as soon as we stop, but whatever you do, don't tell the passengers until then or we'll have chaos."

"*Fuck*! Roger that."

Keegan pulled his phone out of his pocket and Jules watched his fingers fly over the keypad. When he finished he looked at her and his eyes told her how hopeless this situation had become. Her stomach knotted, sweat streaked through her scalp and her insides felt like razor blades were ripping her apart.

"We're taking the boat back to sea to disarm the bombs…or far enough out that the chemical doesn't do as much damage."

Flashes of watching the fire, the smoke, and seeing the second plane rip through the south tower where her mother worked made her gag. She bent over, tried to swallow the bile that choked her, but dry heaved and tasted its bitterness.

Another person she loved was about to be taken from her by terrorists and she didn't know if she'd survive this time. If she didn't go out exactly the same way her parents had too, which was preferable at the moment.

This is what she got for letting herself love someone again. Those men she dated before weren't mistakes, they were chosen intentionally because she knew she'd never be able to love them and have to lose them. Keegan MacDonald had given her no choice but to love him. She hadn't chosen him—fate had chosen him for her. And now he was going to die.

With a wail, she dropped to her knees and hugged herself.

"You can't fall apart on me now, baby. Stay with Bob and Louise, listen for the abandon ship order and get in a life boat. Get as far away as you can and a Navy ship will pick you up. I'll meet you at the harbor after this is over."

No you won't. And if you're going to die, I'm going to die with you. I'll meet you in another life, Keegan MacDonald, but I won't let myself love you again.

CHAPTER TWENTY-EIGHT

Keegan went to the bridge and found Wilson and Garrison working with the crew at the control panel. He forced himself not to look at the bodies against the far wall, or the blood on the white tile beneath his boots.

"SITREP?" he asked, stopping beside Garrison.

"The dog and handler are searching for the devices. Lawrence went with the rest of the team to find the missing tango. We're trying to figure out how to turn this bitch around, because the Captain, Staff Captain and 1st Officer are dead. The Safety Officer and Chief Security Officer are getting the life boats and crew ready for the bells."

The woman beside Gars glanced back over her shoulder at him. "I'm the 2nd Officer, but I'm new. This is my first time doing this outside of a simulator and that was on a different vessel, and not at speed. I need to make sure I get this right or we'll stall or ground the ship."

"What's the make of this ship? Type of engine?" Keegan asked, pulling out his phone.

She spouted off the specifications and he texted Greg to find someone who could call on the ship to shore radio to give her instructions. This needed to happen fast, because it wouldn't be long until they reached Edgewater.

The control room door opened and Keegan groaned when Jules strode in, her face ravaged, but determined. His stomach fell when his phone dinged. He looked, and instead of a reply from the Commander, it was a no service alert.

"Where's your ship to shore phone?" he asked, the hair on the back of his neck raising.

The 2nd Officer reached a few feet away to pick up the handset. She turned to hand it to him. Keegan keyed it, but it was obviously inoperable.

"They've disabled coms," he said, his heart taking a plunge to his stomach. "This had to just happen because I just had a text go through an hour ago." He handed the phone back to the officer. "Where's the coms center on this ship?"

"Two decks down—forward. There's a control room behind the stairs," she replied.

"Get this thing turned around!" Keegan shouted as he took off running, because he thought he had just found their unaccounted for tango.

He heard other feet squeaking on the tile floor behind him as he pushed through the door, but he wasn't letting her distract him. He found the stairs beside the bridge and flew down them two at a time. His heart pounded as he ran two decks down and found the control room door. Pistol in hand, he grabbed the handle and flung it open and a dark-skinned man in navy blue crew coveralls turned and fired at him. Keegan dove and his right shoulder drove into the deck when he landed. Red-hot pain blinded him as he reached for his pistol with his left hand.

Before he could, a shot rang out and he flinched as he waited for the blackness of death to claim him.

When it didn't come, he opened his eyes and saw a red-haired angel standing above him, aiming into the control room.

"I thought I told you to stay in the suite," he growled, his blood running cold at the thought that she could've taken the bullet meant for him.

"You might be used to leaving your partner behind, but that's not how I operate. I'd say that's a good thing wouldn't you?" Jules snarled back, melting him into the deck with her eyes.

"Go back to the room, Jules," he grated as he sat up and held his arm to his side.

Instead of listening, she pushed the metal door back and walked inside the room. When she came back out with a small black box, her hand shook as she held it out to him in her palm.

"Is this what you were looking for?" she asked, her voice choked and her eyes wild.

Keegan vaulted up to grab it from her before she dropped it. "Yes, this looks like the detonator." And it also appeared the bombs were on a joint timer and that time was ticking.

One hour, ten minutes and twenty-four seconds.

"Get my pistol and his, and meet me on the bridge," Keegan said, striding to the stairway with adrenaline mixing with bile to make him want to vomit.

This was not a manual detonation device. The timers on the bombs had already been activated. Since the second tango told them the bombs would blow if the ship stopped, Keegan would bet his left nut there was a secondary mechanism in the engine room to detonate them if the engines fell below a certain RPM.

He had to get this information to the assist team *now*. When he walked back into the wheelhouse, he swayed back toward the door when the engine revved and the ship swayed hard to the left.

"*Don't* slow down!" he yelled as he staggered over to the master panel. "Full speed turn, or we're going to have problems."

"What's up?" Wilson asked. "Why in the hell did you run out of here so fast?"

"The tango is down and this is the detonator," Keegan said, holding it out to him.

"A timer?" he asked, looking confused. "I thought this was supposed to be a manual detonation? Isn't that what the tango you interrogated said?"

"No, he said if the ship stops, the bomb explodes," Keegan corrected. "Which means—"

"There's a secondary trigger tied to the engine!" Gars shouted and the ten crew members gathered at the control panel turned terrified eyes his way.

The engine revved higher, the boat groaned as it leaned far right, and he looked at the 2nd Officer. With a look of determination, she jammed a switch forward, twisted a knob, and the bow of the ship pirouetted to the left.

He imagined all of the passengers knew now that something was wrong, since they were all probably thrown across the deck when she whipped the ship around. He just hoped none of them were hurt, because this adventure was far from over.

"Do we have com with the assist team?" Keegan asked.

"Yes, they've found two of the devices," Garrison replied, handing him a radio. "I'm going down there to help them find the third. You and Wilson stay up here to keep us at speed…and pray. You might want to make an announcement and lie to the passengers so we don't have a riot to deal with too."

CHAPTER TWENTY-NINE

Jules opened the bridge door and walked in on shaky legs. How she was walking at all was a mystery to her. Being locked up in that suite wasn't helping anything, so she went to find Keegan and demand he include her. Now, she was so glad she hadn't stayed where she was put. He hadn't said thank you, but she'd bet he wanted to.

She handed Keegan his pistol and he tucked it into his waistband.

"What can I help with? And don't tell me to go back to the suite or I'll punch you in the balls, Boris," she said, feeling eyes on her from the crew at the master panel.

"I need you to make an announcement for me to explain why we just turned the ship on a dime to head back out to sea. A lie of course, because I've got nothing," Keegan replied, surprising her. "We need the passengers to remain calm, and you are in charge of making sure they stay that way until we call all clear."

Or until we all end up as space dust, she thought, and nausea swirled in her gut as fear tried to consume her again. "I can do that. We've had an engine problem and can't block the channel if the ship stalls."

The corner of his mouth ticked up and the other followed. "Oh, you're good," he said, looking relieved.

"I have my talents and lying happens to be one of them." *Mostly to myself, but whatever.* "Shooting is the second talent, so remember that."

"Thank you for saving my bacon, Agent Lawson. I'm glad you had my six," he replied, his pain-filled eyes softening. He reached up to rub his bicep. "Fixing my shoulder is another of your talents, so could you *please* have someone get me an ice pack?"

If he was asking for an ice pack he must be hurting something fierce, because she almost had to fight the stubborn ass last night to do ice therapy.

"I can do that, too. Anything else?" she asked.

"Yeah, a kiss for luck," he said, his head descending toward hers. At the last minute she turned her face and his lips branded her cheek.

Jules was the unluckiest person in the world, so he wouldn't be finding good fortune for himself on her lips or anywhere else. She was not going to let him start things she knew he wouldn't be given a chance to finish. As soon as the all clear came, if it came, she was getting off this boat and away from Keegan MacDonald as fast as her legs would carry her.
She'd let him get too close to her, which probably explained why they were in this situation.

Fate could go get fucked—she was done with the fickle, game-playing bitch forever. Jules was at peace with her solitary life, where grief didn't exist.

"Are you okay?" he asked, tipping her chin up to meet her eyes.

"You want the truth or a lie?" she asked, and he frowned when she pulled her chin from his grasp. "Yeah, everything is just fine. Now, excuse me while I make an announcement to calm the savage beasts on deck."

199

Emotion made her head swell as she walked over to the master panel. "How do I make an announcement?" she asked the pretty brunette officer at the helm.

She reached down by her thigh and pulled up a microphone, then pushed a few buttons before handing it to her. "Just depress the button on the side."

Jules took the mic, swallowed hard then depressed the button.

"Attention, ladies and gentlemen. We apologize for the sharp U-turn we just made and hope it didn't frighten anyone. We've had minor engine trouble and have to turn back to sea for an hour or so, while the crew fixes the problem. Please stay calm and go to your nearest bar station for free drinks, courtesy of the Radiant Seas Cruise Line." Muted cheers rose outside the thick glass window that overlooked the deck.

She handed back the mic to the female officer who grinned at her. "Nice job—I think I'm going to speak to the line about hiring you when this is over."

"Once I'm off this ship I'm never stepping foot on a cruise ship again, but thank you," Jules replied with a laugh.

"She's right, you rock, babe," Wilson said, walking over to grab her by the shoulders before he jerked her up to kiss her hard on the mouth. She laughed when he set her back on her feet, but when she turned Keegan was glaring at her.

"I'll be back in a minute with your ice pack," she said, as she walked past him to open the door, feeling his eyes burning into her back.

Jules made her way down the steps to the main deck and turned right, but staggered back when she slammed into someone. She met the flat, black eyes of the man who'd been with Abdel Nour on the ship—his lieutenant. Her insides froze as her hand drifted to her weapon, but he bowed and she remembered he wouldn't recognize her. He hadn't ever visited the bar with Abdel.

"Excuse me, madam, is this the bridge?" he said in perfect English with a British-tinged accent, shocking her. "I was just going up, since this is my last chance to take the Captain up on his offer of a tour." His smile made her skin crawl and she noticed a large bulge under the right side of his windbreaker.

You might be going up, but you won't be coming back down.

"Yes, it's at the top of the stairs," she replied, pointing up the stairs. "I'm sure you'll enjoy the tour. It's very interesting to see the inner workings." Jules stepped aside and smiled as she waved her hand to give him access to the stairs. When he was two steps up, she patted her pockets. "Oh, I forgot my cell phone up there, so I'll just come up with you."

His face pinched as he nodded and turned to walk up the stairs. Jules hurried to get behind him and pulled her pistol. He opened the door and she shoved it into his back.

"Drop whatever you have under your right arm," she growled and he tensed.

201

His elbow snapped back and clipped her jaw and Jules' head bounced off the door hard. Stunned, she slid down the door to sit, he spun, and suddenly she was staring down the barrel of an automatic rifle.

Jules rolled as he fired and a fierce roar echoed in her head. When she looked back, Keegan plowed into him and drove him into the glass wall hard enough to shatter it. The weapon skated across the floor, Wilson dove for it, and came up with it aimed at the terrorist.

Keegan and the man struggled until he threw him on the ground, pounced on top of him and commenced pounding his face with his left fist. When he stopped to grab the back of his skull and his chin, Wilson walked over there and put his hand on Keegan's shoulder.

"That's enough, dude—he's unconscious," he said, and Keegan stopped to look down at the man as he drew in ragged breaths. "Let him rot in prison with Abdel. The devil doesn't want him."

The radio on Keegan's belt alerted. "Two down, one to go. Third is in a locked freezer in the port kitchen and we're working on it," a brusque, masculine voice announced, and three-quarters of the starch left Jules body. The other quarter was reserved for when they disabled the third bomb and this nightmare could be over.

Jules' breath came out in a rush as she laid on the cool tile floor and prayed that would be soon. When this was over, she would be thankful to get back to her white-collar criminals. She'd leave fighting terrorists to heroes like Keegan, Wilson, Lawrence, and Garrison, who had no problem giving up the last of their nine lives to the cause. They worked for God, and He could have them. Jules just wanted to be a mortal again.

CHAPTER THIRTY

"Oh, *God*, tell me you're okay, baby…" Keegan groaned, sounding sick, as he knelt beside her and skimmed his left hand down her back.

Before she could answer, he rolled her over and did the same on her front side. Wilson knelt on her other side, but when he put his hand on her middle, Keegan pushed him away.

"Hands off—I've got this!" he growled, glaring at his buddy.

"Do I need to call up a medic for both of you?" Wilson asked, staring at Keegan's right arm, which he had cradled across his stomach. His left hand was cut up badly from interaction with the terrorist's teeth she'd imagine.

"No, but you might want to call one for him. We need him breathing so he can talk," Keegan said, shooting a glance at the man lying unconscious by the wall. "This won't be done until all of them are in custody or dead."

"I'm not worried about him, and you shouldn't be either. The feds will find them all. We just need to finish our part and get off this boat."

Jules couldn't agree more. When the radio on Keegan's belt keyed again her whole body tensed, and his did too.

"Third device is clear. All clear. Notifying command, so start evac." The voice on the radio sounded as relieved as Jules felt. Her whole body shook with it. She looked up into Keegan's eyes and they glistened as he pulled her up to his chest for a tight, one-armed squeeze and she realized he was shaking too. Hot tears burned her eyes as he released her.

They'd made it out alive.

He turned to the 2nd Officer. "Great job, Sharon—stop the ship and sound the bells to offload the passengers into lifeboats. I imagine the Navy will board to gather evidence and safely remove the devices, before bringing the ship into the harbor, so the crew should go too."

Jules sat up and noticed as soon as the woman flipped a series of switches, her body shook violently before she disappeared from view. With a growl, Wilson left her and ran over there to help Sharon.

When he pulled her up to her feet, she brushed off his hand and grabbed the mic. She pushed a button on the dashboard and five sharp bells rang.

"Attention passengers and crew, this is your 2nd Officer—although there is no present danger, thanks to the brave men and women who have contained a threat we had on board, we need you to *immediately* move to your muster stations to board life boats. Do *not* go back to your cabins to retrieve personal items—move calmly to your muster stations, *now*. You may contact the Radiant Seas Line to collect your belongings once the ship is safely back in harbor." She pressed a button, then hung up the mic, but the message and bells continued to repeat.

Jules was surprised when Sharon threw herself against Wilson and hugged him like he was her life ring. He put his arms around her, glanced at Keegan and grinned. The bridge door opened and Lawrence and Garrison strode in looking haggard.

"*Fuck*, that was too close," Gars said, huffing a breath. "Ten minutes to spare? Those bomb techs have nerves of freaking steel."

Jules had zero nerves left. They were all worn down to nubs.

"Can you two take out the trash?" Keegan asked, glancing at the jihadi who was now moving and groaning. "Get the other one in the suite, too. I'm sure Homeland will be boarding with our guys so you can turn them over. I'm going to make sure Bob, Louise, and Jules, get on a raft, then I'll find you."

"We're on it," Lawrence replied, walking that way with Garrison on his heels.

Keegan held out his left hand to help Jules up, but she shook her head and got up on her own. "So you're not going with us?" she asked, both disappointed and relieved.

That would make things easier for her, so why did her heart twist so hard when she met his eyes? She looked away because she knew he'd see her regrets. Even at this last minute, she was reconsidering her decision.

Keegan MacDonald was a good and loving man and she had fallen hard and fast in love with him. But his career choice was a deal-breaker. Even though he was retired from the military, he was still active duty for some counter-terror organization. The world needed men like him, but she didn't need to love one of them.

"No, I have to stay here to give a SITREP to the boarding party. The Navy will pick you up from the life raft and make sure you get to shore. I'll catch up with you when I'm relieved."

"And *God*—your *boss*—will want a SITREP, too. Don't forget *Him*." She sighed, and batted her burning eyes. "I guess you're never going to tell me who you really work for." *And if you were in my life, you'd continue to keep things from me, like how much danger you're really in when He calls you up.*

"I'm sorry, I still can't, baby," he said, putting his hand on her face to stroke her cheek with his thumb. The tender gesture made her look into his soulful gray eyes and the raw emotion she saw there dragged words to her lips she would never utter. She bit her lower lip to keep them right where they belonged.

Loving this man and leaving him now would be much easier than loving him and losing him. She'd lost too many people she loved in her life to take a chance on a man who sought out situations to get himself killed.

Controlled adventure in life was a good thing, she wanted those adventures to remind herself she was alive. What she didn't want was to live with a different kind of terror every day, fear that he'd get into another situation like this one and not be so lucky. He would die and leave her to die a slow and agonizing death inside, while she was still alive.

That almost happened when her parents and her brother died. Then again when her grandmother left her.

It had taken Jules a long time to finally get past the pain and feel alive inside again. She was not a masochist and that was not the type of pain she would subject herself to again voluntarily.

She forced herself to laugh, but it almost sounded like a whimper. "I guess this is goodbye then, Boris. You take care of yourself," she said, her voice trembling as she tiptoed to press her lips to his. "I can't say it's been fun, but it has been an adventure I'll never forget."

And one I'll never repeat.

CHAPTER THIRTY-ONE

"I don't know why she left," Keegan growled, when Bob asked yet again. He'd been asking daily for the last month. "I can't read her mind, but I know one thing. I'm not chasing another woman. Those days are over for me, Unk."

"Look at me, dumbass!" Bob shouted, and Keegan dropped the wrench back in the toolbox, then looked up to meet his uncle's eyes with a sigh. "Did you tell her you love her?"

"No, because I don't," Keegan replied, flinching when a sharp pain sliced through the center of his chest. He didn't *want* to, but fuck if he didn't. He'd get over it, though, just like he had with Cee Cee. He wasn't in any more pain than he'd been in before he met Jules Lawson.

"And you are a fucking liar. I know love when I see it, boy—I've been living it daily for nearly twenty-five years. Louise is my rudder and I'd be lost without her."

Keegan threw back his head and groaned. "Even if I did, she didn't give me a chance to say it, because she didn't want to *hear* it!"

"Maybe it's something else. Did you say something to piss her off? I know she was pretty angry that you locked her in that cabin with us."

Anger and frustration rushed up to make his head feel like it would explode. "She's *gone*, so just leave it alone! We had a *fling*—it's *over*!" Keegan scrubbed his hand over his mouth, because the words tasted like acid on his tongue.

"Have you seen the doctor about that surgery?"

Bob demanded, harping on his second favorite topic, since he and Louise went with him to the ER after he left the ship. "A one-armed mechanic is about as useless to me as you are without her."

Keegan's anger turned to rage and consumed him as he shot up to his feet. His fists curled and he hissed a breath reaching up to massage his right shoulder.

"If I'm useless to you, Unk, then I won't waste any more of your fucking time," he growled as he spun and stalked toward the back door.

"You're not wasting my time—you're wasting your own, Son. Stop being a stubborn ass. Have the surgery, and go get that girl. If you don't, you'll be useless for the rest of your life. You need a rudder, boy, because you're headed for the rocks."

Keegan pushed the back door open and the bright sunlight blinded him. Bob's words echoed inside his skull, his heart pounded and his ears rang. A feeling of hopeless desperation kept him from walking out. If he walked through that door, he had no idea where he'd go, what he'd do, or how he'd survive. He would be headed for the rocks with no job, no family who gave a shit about him, and nowhere to live.

He had a little money, so he could find a place closer to his parents in Tennessee, but they were still angry at him for turning his back on his brother. He might be able to make peace with them and Kane, but what then? He would live in a small Podunk town on his disability and have no purpose in life. He'd shrivel up and die inside.

That was the scariest consequence of all and what kept him planted right where he was.

Bob had offered him a purpose and by walking out, he was spitting in his uncle's face. Without the surgery, his uncle was right, he would be useless here. Taking a deep breath, he blew it out slowly and let the door close. He turned around to face Bob and his insides clenched seeing the disappointment on his face.

"I'll make the appointment to see the surgeon today and schedule the surgery as soon as possible," he said, and his uncle nodded.

"And the girl?" Bob asked, not letting Keegan off the hook.

"I'll try to give her a call to at least find out why she left," Keegan said with a sigh. "But I can't guarantee anything there. I really do think I was just a heat-of-the-moment thing for her."

But it definitely wasn't for him. To satisfy his uncle, he would make the call and have her tell him to his face it was just about sex to her. It would hurt worse than his shoulder did now, but maybe it would be cathartic and help him find closure, too. Put those fantasies of her calling him out of the blue to tell him she loved him too right out of his mind.

***

"Hey, Keeg—how are you feeling, baby?" a female voice cooed, as soft fingers brushed across his forehead to push his hair back to drag him up a long dark tunnel.

He opened blurry eyes, saw red hair and excitement rushed through him, but when they focused, Louise appeared. With a groan, he closed them and his shoulder throbbed. He tried to move his fingers and nothing. Panic shot through him as he shot up but was pulled back down to the bed by the tubes connected to his body.

"Is my arm still there?" he asked, his voice raw as pressure built in his head and his insides went numb. Losing a limb had been more of a fear than dying on missions. He'd seen how some of his buddies went home and would rather be dead.

Not riding a bike again would kill him.

When he tried to ride his bike home after the cruise ship was hauled into harbor, it was too excruciating to extend his arm and his hand was too weak to grip the throttle, so Bob had to ride it home and he rode with Louise in the Jeep. He hadn't ridden since, because it hurt too fucking bad and never riding again had been a fear he'd secretly dealt with since.

"Settle down. You're loopy on the drugs, and of course your arm is still there. The doc said your entire arm will be numb for two or three days from the anesthesia, and when the feeling comes back it will hurt like hell for months," Louise said, holding his shoulder to the bed.

"I rather the pain so I know it's there," Keegan replied, as relief made him weak and he reached up to feel the thick gauze bandages and moved his hand down his padded arm to the sling, which tied his forearm across his middle.

"Doc said he had a lot of repair work to do in there, but he thinks you'll have pretty close to full mobility after several months of intensive physical therapy."

Keegan's eyes snapped to her. "*Really?* The other doctor didn't say that. He said I'd be lucky to have fifty-percent after it's healed." He tried like hell not to let that hope inside him, because he knew he was just setting himself up for a helluva fall.

Just like he had with thinking Jules would return his calls.

During the week he waited for surgery, he'd left message after message for her. He'd texted her and knew she'd seen them—at least the first five or so he'd sent. Then he figured she'd blocked him because the time stamps stopped.

That told him what he needed to know.

Emotion built again, his chest tightened, but Keegan forced himself to relax.

She was just a woman, and they were a dime a dozen. At least the kind he planned to allow into his world from here on out were. That other part of him was dead now, as dead as his arm was at the moment and it wasn't all that bad, so far.

He would just deal with the pain Louise said would come once the numbness wore off.

213

Like the grueling PT he'd have to endure for his arm to get better, he'd do other things, and other women, to wipe a certain blue-eyed blonde turned temporary redhead from his mind. He knew now he'd been as temporary in her life as that red hair color.

He'd done what he promised Bob, and it was over. If he brought her up again, Keegan would shut him down fast. Jules Lawson was a closed subject.

"Where's Uncle Bob?" he asked.

Louise's face flushed. "He had some errands to run, but he'll be here soon. I need to call him and tell him you're awake."

Louise stood and hurried out of the room with her phone in her hand. Keegan closed his eyes, and sighed. He was thankful for the IV that pumped drugs into his body as he floated on a white cloud and found peace. He hoped they gave him plenty of scripts to take home with him so he could get through the next few months.

A soft, warm palm cupped his cheek and he smiled as he turned his head toward it and nuzzled the silky skin. A very familiar floral scent drifted up his nostrils and when his mind connected the scent with who it belonged to, he jerked his face away and opened his eyes.

"Hey, Boris," Jules said, her eyes glistening as she pulled her hand away.

Keegan's eyes soaked her up and his insides unfurled as hot need roasted his gut, melting the ice around his heart. He glanced at the drip bag and wondered if he was hallucinating from the drugs. But when he looked back at her, he knew she was really standing beside the bed.

She reneged on your agreement, MacDonald. She gave you the kiss-off when you needed her and didn't return your calls. You don't need her, or her sympathy. Don't give her another chance to stab you in the gut.

"What the fuck are you doing here, Jules?" he growled, but his question was answered when he saw Bob standing behind her.

"Bob said you needed me. So, here I am," she replied, her voice trembling. "You said I was good at fixing shoulders."

And breaking hearts. No, he didn't need a damned thing from her. She'd done enough damage.

Keegan whipped his eyes toward the wall because if he looked at her one second longer the roar building in his chest might just escape.

"Bob was mistaken. I don't need a damned thing from you, so you can leave. I'm sure you have better things to do," he grated, his left fist curling to combat the pressure in his chest.

"I'm transferring to the Los Angeles office in a few months, so I have some time off. I really would like to help you get through this," she said, and Keegan ground his teeth to dust.

"Why, Natasha? *Why* do you want to help me?" he asked, forcing his eyes back to hers.

215

She flinched and didn't respond for a second. "Because we're friends and I care about you, MacDonald," she finally replied.

"I have plenty of friends, you've met them. I don't *need* another friend, Agent Lawson—I told you that." A tremor shook her and her face flushed, but she didn't refute her statement. He looked at the wall again. "Go to Los Angeles, Jules. I know you're probably already compiling a list of terror suspects to take down. Have at them, but don't call me to help. I'll probably be out of the country with my friends."

"You're going back to the teams?" she asked, the fear in her tone real. "But Bob said you were taking over at the—" she stopped on a whimper to glance over her shoulder at Bob, whose face was grim. When her eyes found Keegan's again, they were filled with terror.

"The doc says I'll likely have full mobility after I heal, so yes, I'll be rejoining the teams if they'll have me. That is where I belong."

Those men were his family and from here on out they were all he needed.

CHAPTER THIRTY-TWO

Jules took the last sip of her cold coffee and cringed as she stood to go get a refill. She needed to bring the whole pot into the temporary office where she was working, because jet lag was kicking her ass. Flying cross-country, then having to report at nine a.m. should be illegal.

Packing up a houseful of memories to sell a house should be, too. That had taken two months because parting with each thing her grandmother held dear, putting each happy photo of their family before 2001 into a box, had chipped away a piece of her soul.

But she had to do it, because moving it all to California was too expensive, and focusing on her grief wouldn't allow her the fresh start she needed.

Los Angeles wouldn't have been her pick for assignments, but it beat being stuck in Idaho, the second option she was given when she returned to the Financial Crimes Division and requested a transfer out of Virginia. She couldn't surf in the snowstorms and knew the winters in Idaho would just depress her more.

A sharp pain sliced through her sternum and she rubbed it with a fist as she walked down the hallway to the kitchen area. Surfing brought him to her mind every time and she figured embracing the pain by hitting the waves would help her get rid of it. Her plan was to surf that man right out of her mind. It was going to take a lot of board time to get past his brutal rejection, but Jules was determined.

Saying goodbye to Bob and Louise had been

tough. They didn't want to let her leave—begged her to stay and try again, but Jules had no doubt she'd done the right thing by walking away from a man who could destroy her if she let him.

It will go away—you will get over this.

Her mantra for the last few months still didn't make it better. But it would eventually, if she kept repeating it like she had before. Jules reached for the half-empty pot and was surprised how badly her hand shook as she filled her cup.

"Good morning, Natasha," a deep masculine voice said behind her and she sloshed coffee all over the counter and her hand. She set the pot down on the counter and felt dizzy as she moved to the sink to run cold water over the burn.

"What are you doing here and how did you find me, Boris?" she grumbled, but her heart felt like it suddenly had wings.

"I'm here to find out why you left me at the harbor, and why you didn't return my calls. I need to hear it from you, not Uncle Bob. Right now, I don't believe a thing he says," Keegan said, his voice harsh.

Jules turned off the tap, but braced her arms on the sink and kept her head down, until she was sure she had control of the tears that wanted pour down her face. She sucked in a sharp breath, then turned to face him.

Her eyes ate up his handsome, pinched face and her heart soared higher, until she met his intense stare and saw derision there, which brought her back to earth. He was only here to find out if his uncle lied to him and probably get answers that he wouldn't believe anyway.

No matter what she said, he would be going back in the military. But she owed it to Bob to vindicate him.

"Your Uncle Bob is a good man who cares about you and he was just trying to help." She folded her arms over her chest, to compress the pain. "He lied to me too, but I know his heart was in the right place."

"His heart was in *my* business, where it definitely doesn't belong," Keegan snarled, his jaw working as he ground his teeth. "I love him with everything I have, but that doesn't give him license to meddle in my life."

"What does it give him license to do? Sit by and watch you destroy yourself?" she asked with a snort, and his eyes narrowed. "You should be thankful you have someone in your life to love you and care whether you live or die."

"Oh yeah, your dead family," he said, his voice heavy with snark as he took a step toward her. "Death is part of living, Natasha. How long will you use that as an excuse not to let anyone get close enough to love you? You're going to die a lonely old woman."

Emotion choked her, and her eyes filled too fast to stop the tears from flowing down her face. "And you're going to die a young man who never let himself slow down long enough to enjoy love. You'll live from one adrenaline fix to another until you go out in a blaze of glory and leave whoever is foolish enough to love you behind to grieve." Her lower lip trembled. "I can't let

myself love you, MacDonald, because if you died, I
wouldn't survive this time."

He swiped at her tears with his left hand, and a
shuddering sigh shook her.

"Well, I didn't want to *let* myself love you either.
But you crashed into my life and made it impossible for
me *not* to love you. We need to figure out how to fix this
ourselves, Jules. If we can't, I'll walk away but I'm here to
try," he said, his voice vibrating with sincerity. "You want
me to forget about trying to get back on the teams? Call
God and resign from his team, too? If so, I will do that.
For you. But I need you to tell me, if I do that, you'll
never walk away from me again. That you'll talk to me
instead of running, because I won't be chasing you again."

Something inside Jules broke loose and almost
brought her to her knees, as a wail floated to her lips. "I
don't want to ruin your life, Keegan. I love you enough to
let you do what makes you happy. If that's being on the
teams, I won't ask you to quit for me. I just can't be with
you if that's your choice. We can still be friends—"

He made a loud, abrasive sound like a game show
buzzer and pinned her to the counter with his body.
Coffee seeped into the back of her skirt but she didn't
care as she stared into his sizzling eyes.

"That's not an option, remember? My terms
haven't changed since the first time I stated them. I don't
want a friend, or a sometimes lover. I want a relationship
with strings thick enough to tie you to my dock forever. I
have it on good authority that I need a rudder and I want

you to be that woman. If that's not something *you* want—
let me know now."

"I love you, Boris and would be honored to be
your rudder," Jules said, her insides going liquid with love.
His mouth glided toward hers and when their lips met,
her soul reached for his and she finally found her safe
harbor.

EPILOGUE

"I can't believe you made me pay for the honeymoon. You are making money hand over fist at the shop now. I know because I'm keeping the books," Jules said, and Keegan bit back a laugh as she buried the end of her board in the sand. He planted his board beside hers and his eyes locked on the hem of her short, terry robe when the breeze lifted it, giving him a quick glimpse of paradise.

"Hey, you promised me an all-expense paid trip to Tortola to surf. Watch what you promise, beautiful, because I *will* hold you to them," Keegan replied.

That included being with him forever, which she promised in Virginia behind their new beach house yesterday. Keegan didn't need adrenaline fixes anymore, because he knew every day of the rest of his life would be a new adventure with this woman.

"But I *didn't* promise to do *this*," she hissed, tightening the robe belt. God, she was cute when she was agitated, but her glittering eyes said she was as titillated as he was right now.

"But you put the thought in my mind, Natasha, so it's your fault it has starred in my fantasies since that moment." He dropped a beach towel on the sand then sat on it. "Consider it my wedding present," he said looking up at her with a grin.

"So when will I get *my* wedding present?" she asked, poking out her lip, making him want to bite it. "You've been teasing me about it for a week."

Teasing her was another of his new favorite pastimes, because her methods of trying to make him talk were incredible. He was thankful she reserved her knife-to-the-balls move for terrorists. A helmet with Keegan's Bitch written on it had nothing on this gift though.

"Tonight, and *I* promise you will love it," he replied, his smile widening. He'd smiled so much lately his damned cheeks hurt. Her eyes fixed on his mouth and she licked her lips. After eight months together, he could almost read her mind. She wanted to have sex right now to distract him from what they were here for to get out of this.

Not happening, baby.

"Don't look at me like that until after you come back," he said, and her face flushed.

He leaned back on his elbows to watch her and his shoulder twinged, but it was so much better he barely noticed. He was back to eighty-five percent mobility now, and the therapist said if he kept working out like he had been, he might just hit ninety soon. So now, he could lift his smoking-hot wife and carry her to bed, work, and ride his bike. All he cared about now.

"Someone is going to *see* me! They will videotape this and it will end up on YouTube. If that happens, I will kill you," she growled, her eyes sparkling as she pointed a finger at him.

"If you kill me, I won't be around to give you your present tonight," he said, rubbing his chronically hard cock.

When she rolled her eyes and unfastened her belt he laughed, but his smile faded when she dropped the robe at her feet and walked bare-assed to jerk her board out of the sand. This little trick could backfire, he thought, fighting the urge to tell her he'd changed his mind and carry her into the copse of palm trees to try out sex in the hammock there.

"It's Tuesday. The guy at the front desk who told me about this place assured me it's only a weekend hangout for the hedonistic crowd."

"That guy will die, then, if anyone shows up," she said, turning back to face him with her board under her arm.

The sight of her curvy, naked body backlit by the bright sun, her wispy blonde hair blowing in the tropical breeze, and every inch of her deliciously tanned skin on optimal display stole his breath. His fantasies had nothing on this reality.

"I changed my mind. Let's go try out the hammock," he growled, as he pushed up to his feet. Her full lips curled as she shook her head.

"Too bad, SEAL Boy. I'm doing this now. Don't

dare me to do things and expect *me* not to follow through," she said.

"But what if it ends up on YouTube, babe?" he asked, not really liking that idea now. This woman was *his* and if anyone touched her, he would and *could* kill them now.

"If it ends up on YouTube, every man on the planet, including your horny buddies, will be ogling your wife. Think about that before you issue another challenge." She smiled and it hit him right in the chest. "You asked for this and it could be the wedding gift that keeps on giving."

With a laugh, she turned and ran into the surf and he stood there stunned as he watched her carry her board to the second cut, before she laid on it to paddle. He wanted to be that board right then, to have her oily body sliding all over him. Fuck, he was a moron for not choosing the hammock first, he thought adjusting himself.

When she reached the fourth cut, she turned her board toward the beach and Keegan held his breath as she pushed up and her board rose on the horizon with the swell of the wave. She gripped the edge, pushed up to put her feet under her. The wave crested and she stood to gracefully ride the peak, twisting her hips to keep the board under her.

The sun glistened on her skin, the frothy white

foam danced under her board as the perfect wave carried a sea goddess toward him. Neptune's beautiful daughter turned mortal, a gift from the King himself for his end of watch.

The perfect woman for him.

If you enjoyed **Slow Ride**, I'd greatly appreciate you leaving a review for me where you purchased your copy. Hot SEAL hero Keegan MacDonald first appeared in the third book in my Deep Six Security series, HELL BENT. If you'd like to read more about him before he met Jules, you can find it here: www.books2read.com/HellBent

The Sleeper SEALs series is a multi-author branded series which includes twelve standalone books by some of your favorite romantic suspense authors. You can check out the rest of the books in the series on our website: www.SleeperSEALs.com/series-books or click the links below.

Susan Stoker – PROTECTING DAKOTA – 9/5/17
Becky McGraw – SLOW RIDE – 9/26/17
Dale Mayer – MICHAELS' MERCY – 10/3/17
Becca Jameson – SAVING ZOLA – 10/17/17
Sharon Hamilton – BACHELOR SEAL – 10/31/17
Elle James – MONTANA RESCUE – 11/14/17
Maryann Jordan – THIN ICE – 11/28/17
Donna Michaels – GRINCH REAPER – 12/12/17
Lori Ryan – ALL IN – 1/9/18
Geri Foster – BROKEN SEAL – 1/23/18
Elaine Levine – FREEDOM CODE – 2/6/18
J.m. Madden – FLAT LINE – 2/20/18

To keep up with my upcoming releases, get advance sneak peeks at covers and exclusive excerpts and contests, please join my newsletter:
http://bit.ly/2vMzIte

To find more of my edge-of-your-seat romantic suspense novels, please check out my **Deep Six Security series here**: http://authorbeckymcgraw.com/deep-six-security-series/

All of the books in the Deep Six Security series have crossover characters, but can be read as standalone novels. Here's a little sample from **Gray Matter: Deep Six Security Book 5**, my latest release in the series.

Gray Matter Universal Buy Link:
http://www.books2read.com/GrayMatter

PROLOGUE

"Uncle Vinny?" Mickie called as she walked into the too-quiet office at Girabaldi Enterprises on Friday morning at nine-thirty. When there was no answer, her brow knotted as she put her purse down beside her desk, then leaned around the corner to glance down the hallway.

The light was on in her uncle's office and the door ajar, so he *had* to be in there. Vinny *never* left his door unlocked when he wasn't in, because his safe was in the closet. She strode down the hall and frowned when she passed her cousin Teresa's office and found the light was still off.

She was thankful to see it, because that meant her reaming from her cousin for being thirty minutes late would not happen until she had her latte, but it was odd. Teresa was never late, but then she'd never left sick before either, and she had yesterday afternoon during a heated argument Vinny was having with an associate. But her arms and bags had been loaded down with work when she left, of course.

Mickie had no idea what the argument was about, because Vinny and Teresa didn't include her in their business dealings, but she heard every word. It was that loud. She didn't ask questions, because she didn't want to know. She was perfectly happy being the oblivious office worker, errand girl, and barista here, who was given as much notice as the potted plant beside her desk. She was paid well to keep her nose in her own business, and she did.

Hear no evil. See no evil. Speak no evil. Get a paycheck.
Stopping at her uncle's office door, Mickie pushed

229

it open wider and walked in, but stopped in her tracks. Her fingers went numb and she dropped her lunch bag. She ran over to drop to her knees beside her uncle, who lay face down on the Persian rug in front of his desk. From the doorway, the red rug masked the red blood that had soaked in all around his head.

Her hand shook as she reached to feel his throat for a pulse. When she didn't find one, she started to try to turn him over, but her eyes landed on a small, charred hole at his hairline, which told her she wouldn't be finding one. The biscotti she'd eaten on the way in lunged up to her throat to choke her as she shrank back to put a violently shaking hand over her mouth.

Her eyes darted to a pistol laying in front of the chairs across from her uncle's desk. It was her uncle's thirty-eight that he kept in his drawer. He must've tried to defend himself, but the gunman shot him first.

What if the killer came back? Mickie's heart raced as she scrambled on her knees toward the chair, but her eyes darted to the open closet door. She saw the light, heard someone ruffling through things in there and froze.

Oh, Dio! The killer was still in that closet!

Mickie grabbed the pistol, but it slipped through her sweaty palms twice before she got a good grip on it. Her hand shook so badly, she dropped it again as she crawled back to her uncle. That told her she would never be able to shoot it at whoever was in that closet anyway, so she left it there.

The best thing she could do was sneak out of there like she'd come in. *Before* whoever was in the closet realized she was there and shot her too! The rug burned Mickie's knees as she race-crawled to the office door and used the door jamb to pull herself to her feet.

Feeling a bullseye between her shoulder blades, she ran on the toes of her stilettos toward the front door and her heart didn't beat once until she was outside. A junky, beat up car on the other side of the lot caught her eye, and her heart stopped again when she saw a head in the passenger side of the vehicle.

God, how could he have missed her going into the office? *How could she have missed that car?!?*

Thank *God* she relied on the bus instead of driving, and that it was later than usual today. Well, she wasn't going to give that lookout another chance to see her, she thought, streaking down the sidewalk, toward the side of the building. When she rounded the corner, she saw her only hiding place in the wide open space would be the garbage bin.

The thought of climbing inside that bin nauseated her, but not enough to make her want to die to avoid it. Mickie ran there, lifted the lid and gagged as the odor of hot garbage surrounded her. She held her breath, stepped up on a cardboard box beside the bin and fell inside on top of the pile of refuse. Eventually she had to breathe, and lost her biscotti for her first few breaths. After an hour or so, she got used to the smell and settled in. Every so often, she'd lift the lid to look down the alley, but she stayed there.

Three hours later, Mickie got brave and decided to go to the corner to see if they had gone. She had to go back inside the office to get her purse and call the police, but she would not be there when they arrived. They would ask questions to which *she* didn't have answers. She knew who did have those answers, but that woman was conveniently absent today.

The day her uncle was murdered.

Mickie was not going to be Teresa's scapegoat. They didn't pay her enough for *that*.

She lifted the lid on the bin, light poured in along with fresh air that reactivated the rank odor, making Mickie gag again. She looked down as she started to climb out and the flowered straps of a familiar canvas tote bag caught her eye. It was obviously the bag that Teresa had used for many years to carry work home with her. One she'd had with her when she left yesterday afternoon.

Mickie stopped, rested the lid on her back so she could see, then pulled the bag out from under the mound of paper it was buried under, which appeared to be company memos and documents, but Mickie was more interested in what was inside the tote. Unzipping it, she spread the sides apart and saw a journal and several notebooks.

The odor inside the dumpster overwhelmed her and alerted her that this was not the place to examine those things. She quickly re-zipped the bag, tossed it to the ground, then climbed out of the dumpster. She would do that in Teresa's office, where she might also find other things that could tell her what was going on here. Before she called the police.

Uncle Vinny was dead, and a few hours wouldn't make him less dead.

Gray Matter - Universal Buy Link:
www.books2read.com/GrayMatter

ABOUT THE AUTHOR

New York Times and USA Today Bestselling Author Becky McGraw writes happily-ever-afters with heat, heart and humor. A Jill of many trades, Becky knows just enough about a variety of subjects to make her contemporary cowboy and romantic suspense novels diverse and entertaining. She resides in Florida with her husband of thirty-plus years, is the mother of three and grandmother of one. Becky is a member of the RWA, Sisters in Crime and Novelists, Inc.

You can contact Becky McGraw here:

Facebook: www.facebook.com/beckymcgrawbooks
Website: www.beckymcgraw.com
Twitter: www.twitter.com/beckymcgrawbook
Email: beckymcgrawbooks@gmail.com
Newsletter: http://bit.ly/2vMzIte

Made in the USA
Coppell, TX
22 April 2020